6 Sexy Stories in 1

Horny

I0683827

Erotica Short Stories, Vol. 9

Just Plain Bob

WARNING

This book contains sexually explicit scenes and adult language. It may be considered offensive to some readers. This book is for sale to adults ONLY.

*   *   *   *   *   *   *   *   *   *   *   *   *   *   *   *   *   *   *

Please store your files wisely where they cannot be accessed by underage readers.

Please feel free to send me an email. Just know that these emails are filtered by my publisher. Good news is always welcome.

Just Plain Bob - **justplainbob@awesomeauthors.org**

About the Publisher

4Fun Publishing, a member of **BLVNP Incorporated**, 340 S. Lemon #6200, Walnut CA 91789, info@blvnp.com / legal@blvnp.com
NOTE: Due to the highly emotional reaction of some people to works of erotic fiction, any email sent to the above address that contains foul language or religious references is automatically deleted by our anti-spam software and will not be seen. All other communications are welcome.

DISCLAIMER

Please don't be stupid and kill yourself. This book is a work of FICTION. Do not try any new sexual practice that you find in this book. It is fiction and not to be confused with reality. Neither the author nor the publisher or its associates assume any responsibility for any loss, injury, death or legal consequences resulting from acting on the contents in this book. Every character in this book is over 18 years of age. The author's opinions are not to be construed as the opinions of the publisher. The material in this book is for entertainment purposes ONLY. Enjoy.

Erotica Short Stories, Vol. 9

HORNY

6 Sexy Stories in 1

By: Just Plain Bob

© Just Plain Bob 2015
ISBN: 978-1-68030-276-9

Table of Contents

-
-
-
-
-
-
-

The Gym

-
-
-
-
-
-
-

I was on the leg press when I saw her come in. Tall woman, I would guess 5'8" or 5'9" and maybe 125 pounds. Blond hair put up in a pony-tail and from the looks of her, I figured that she was there more to stay in shape than to get into shape. She was the kind of woman I liked to see in the circuit machine area – someone easy on the eyes, someone you could watch and appreciate while you worked out.

I finished my three sets on the leg press and was moving to the chest press to work on the anterior deltoids, and triceps when I noticed that she looked a little confused as she stood there looking at the leg extension machine. I walked over to her.

"First time here?"

"Yes."

"You ever use any of these machines before?"

"No. I have a treadmill and a Stairmaster in my basement, but I've never used anything like this before."

"Are you looking to work on a specific area or just a general workout?"

"Just a general workout. The Stairmaster and the treadmill don't do anything for my arms and upper body."

"If you like, I can give you a quick tour and some information on how to use the equipment."

"Do you work here? A personal trainer?"

"No to both. I'm just here for my workout. I remember during my first time here, if someone hadn't taken the time to explain the equipment to me, I could very well have ended up hurting myself. My name is Rob" I said as I extended my hand. She took it and said:

"Minerva, but I prefer to be called Minnie. And yes. I would like it if you showed me around."

I walked her through the circuit training area and explained all the machines to her. I showed her how to adjust the seat, select the weights and gave her a short explanation of what muscle group the machine was designed to work. I pointed out that the machines were numbered and explained that it was best if she used the machines in numerical order.

"They are laid out so you don't keep working the same area over and over. One is for hamstrings, two is for triceps, outer delts and pecs, and three is for quadriceps and so on. Any questions?"

"I'm sure that I'll have dozens once I get started."

She moved to machine number one – the leg press- and started working out and I moved on to finish my workout. I kept looking back at her to see that she was okay (I think I already mentioned that she was easy on the eyes) and she seemed to be getting along okay. I finished my workout, did my stretches and was getting ready to head for the showers when she stopped me.

"Do you work out here often?"

"Every day, Monday through Friday. I'm here when the doors open at five in the morning."

She looked at the wall clock that said three-fifteen and said, "You have been here ten hours?"

I chuckled and said, "No. I was out of town yesterday and I flew in at eleven this morning so today is a late day for me. Nice meeting you Minnie. You take care and hopefully I'll see you around" and then I headed for the shower room.

*****

As he headed for the shower I decided that he would indeed see me around. I hadn't expected to find what I wanted so quickly, but he would do. Fairly good looking, obviously in good shape, no wedding ring – not that that meant anything, after all, hadn't I taken off mine? Yes, he would do nicely. As I watched his tight butt disappear through the door of the men's locker room, I think back on the series of events that brought me – a married woman – to this gym with the prime purpose of picking up a man (and maybe losing that extra ten pounds I didn't want) but make no mistake, the man is what I was after.

I met Brad when he came to work at Chambers Brothers where I was the office manager. He was charming, witty and extremely good looking and when he asked me to have dinner with him, I said yes. It was a fun evening and I said yes to a second date which led to a third and then a fourth, a fifth, and a sixth. I'm not a prude, but I'm not a slut either and I do like sex – a lot – but I really have to like a guy before I give it up and I really liked Brad so on our seventh date he got lucky. In addition to Brad's other good qualities, he turned out to be an excellent lover.

We became a couple and for the next four months we kept steady company. Then disaster struck. I got pregnant. It wasn't supposed to happen, but it did. I couldn't use birth control pills because of some bad side effects, so I depended on diaphragms, spermicides and douching, but it seemed that those methods failed me. My fault, not Brad's since I had told him I was protected. I did what I thought was the right thing and broke up with Brad.

After three weeks of hounding me for the reason of the breakup I finally told him that I was pregnant and he got points for not saying, "Is it mine" or "Are you sure that I'm the father?". Instead, he said that we needed to hurry up and get married so the timing would look right when the baby was born. I told him that we would not be getting married; that I was not going to have a husband who married me out of a sense of obligation. I told him that I had been the one to screw up and I would shoulder the responsibility. He stared at me for several seconds and then walked back to his desk and took something out of his briefcase and then walked back to me. He handed me a little box covered in black velvet and told me to open it. Inside was an engagement ring.

"I was just getting ready to ask you to marry me when you broke it off between us. We can have the license and blood tests out of the way by Thursday, see a justice of the peace on Friday and have the weekend for a honeymoon. What do you say?"

What could I say but yes and it went off as planned. Five months into the pregnancy, I miscarried and there were some complications with the end result that I could never have children. Brad was a little disappointed because he wanted kids, but he told me that it was no biggie, that we could always adopt.

*****

For the next six years, I thought that I had a great marriage and a loving husband. And then I found out that I was probably wrong about that. Brad had left Chambers Brothers for a higher paying position at McFee and Sons. It might have been for more money, but as far as I was concerned it wasn't a better job. It involved a lot of late hours and some traveling which left me home alone with not much else to do but watch idiotic TV shows or read books. I didn't take up any outside hobbies or activities because I wanted to be sure that my time was free so I could spend it with Brad when he was home.

Brad had just returned from a trip and we were attending a promotion party for one of the men he worked with. It was being held at the Marriott and it was my first exposure to the people he worked with. About an hour into the affair I had to use the ladies room. While there I refreshed my makeup, but when I looked in my clutch for my comb it wasn't there. Then I remembered that I had used it in the car and had put it in my coat pocket. I went to the coat room and found my coat hanging on the rack in the back. I was fishing in the pocket for my comb, when I heard a woman's voice just outside the coat room say:

"Did you get a look at Brad's wife?"

"I'll say. After seeing her, I have to wonder what he sees in Alice."

"Do you think she suspects that he is taking Alice to the motel for long lunches?"

"I doubt it. She doesn't look like the type to put up with that kind of crap."

"You're sorry you said no when Brad hit on you? Alice says he is a tiger in the sack."

"No, I'm not sorry. I did consider it for a bit because he is such a hunk, but I decided against it. There is no percentage in playing around with a married man. How about you? Were you tempted?"

"No. I've got a good man at home and even though Brad is like you say – a hunk – I'm not willing to risk what I have for someone who plays around like Brad."

"Knowing Alice, I'm surprised that she hasn't done something tacky like getting buddy-buddy with Brad's wife. You know what I mean?"

"Oh yeah. The old "See how nice I am? I'll bet you don't know I'm screwing your husband" act. I'm pretty sure that Brad had warned her and he probably is watching her pretty close."

"I wonder if her fiancée knows what she is doing?"

"Probably not. He seems to 'gah-gah' over her to see anything but what she wants him to see."

"We had better get back. Don't want to miss the fun if Alice slips by Brad and gets to his wife."

I stood there stunned over what I'd just heard. My Brad cheats on me? No way! It couldn't be my Brad. There had to be another Brad working there. I got my comb out of my coat pocket and went back to the ladies room. I was washing my hands in the sink when a rather brassy looking blonde walked in. She came over next to me and took her lipstick out of her clutch purse. She glanced over at me, smiled, and said:

"You're Brad's wife, right? Minnie is it?"

"That's right."

"I'm Alice. I work with Brad. We have done a lot together since he came to work with us."

"I believe I've heard your name mentioned."

"Well, it is nice meeting you finally. Brad does talk a lot about you when we are together."

"I take it you spend a lot of time together?"

"Oh yes. We are assigned to the same cost center so we end up working a lot of projects together."

"Nice meeting you Alice, but I need to get back to the party."

As I walked out of that restroom, I was no longer saying, "Oh no, not my Brad" but "I wonder if there is anything to what those two women were saying." But it wasn't until I got back to the table and told Brad that I'd met Alice in the bathroom that things took a turn for the worse.

"She told me that she spends a lot of time with you and that you two have done a lot together since you came to work here."

The quick flash of concern (or was it fear) that went across his face pretty much told me that where there was smoke there was likely to be fire. I noticed that for the rest of the night Brad kept glancing nervously at the table where Alice was sitting. I also noticed several people watching our table with bemused grins and smiles on their faces. Did everyone know? Were they thinking "That poor woman, If only she knew" or were they thinking "Way to go Brad, wife and lover in the same room and the wife is clueless."

Brad was quiet on the way home and after several minutes I asked him if something was the matter and he said no; that he was thinking that if he had made the move sooner that would have been his promotion party. I smiled and told him not to worry that he'd get the next promotion.

I kept my suspicions to myself and tried to act normal the rest of the weekend, but it wasn't easy. Brad had been gone four days and he wanted to make love. I was hesitant. I didn't want to make love to him if he was cheating on me, but I really didn't know that he was. I had my suspicions, but that was all. That plus the fact that my refusal would not be normal let me give him what he wanted, but my heart wasn't in it and for the first time in our marriage, Brad didn't bring me to orgasm.

As soon as Brad left for work on Monday, I called into work and arranged to take three days off. I was parked where I could see Brad's car when he came out of the building at lunch time. He had Alice with him. They were laughing and talking as they went over and got in his car. As they pulled out of the parking lot, my heart sank as I began to accept that my husband was a cheating bastard. I pulled out and followed them as they turned on Wilcox and headed south toward motel row. I was debating on whether to wait for them to head for a room or confront him when he got out of the car when his turn signal came on and he pulled into the parking lot at Denny's. I parked across the street and watched as Brad and Alice walked into the restaurant. I started to castigate myself for being a stupid and jealous woman. I should have known that my Brad wasn't going to cheat on me. I followed them back to work and then I did what I always did to relieve stress – I went shopping.

I hit Victoria's Secret, Lane Bryant and a half dozen other places and bought myself some sexy clothes to wear for my hubby when I made it up to him for all the bad thoughts I'd been having.

Before he left for work that morning, Brad told me that he would be working late and while I was a little surer now that he wasn't cheating on me, I still had taken the time off to investigate and I would see it through. More to punish myself for doubting him than for any other reason. At five-thirty Alice came out, got in her car and drove away. I forced myself to sit in my car and watch the building as I told myself:

"You stupid bitch! You should have known better. Sit here, be bored, waste a night because of your stupid idea that Brad was a cheater."

At eight-thirty, Brad came out of the building with two other men and while they were walking to their cars I took off so I could beat Brad home. When he walked in the door, he found me waiting for him in what he called my "fuck suit" - a pair of black pumps with five inch heels and nothing else. I did my absolute best to fuck his brains out.

The next day I was again parked outside where I could see Brad's car. At lunch time, he came out of the building with the same two men I'd seen him in the previous night. I followed them until they turned into the parking lot at The Red Robin and then I went home. I fixed Brad's favorite dinner; put on one of the outfits I'd bought at Victoria's Secret and was waiting just inside the front door when Brad walked into the house at six. I handed him the martini that I had prepared for him (shaken – not stirred) and when he took it from me, I went to my knees, unzipped him and gave him head while he sipped his martini.

Over dinner, he asked me what was the occasion and I told him no special occasion, I just thought things were getting a little stale in the bedroom and needed some spicing up. The night was just as exhausting as the previous one.

Before he left the next morning he told me that it would be another late night for him and not to hold dinner. I smiled at him and told him I would be waiting. Again, more to punish myself for my mistrust than for any other reason. I was outside watching when he and Alice left the building for lunch. I followed along and wondered what restaurant it would be that day. Brad's right turn signal came on and I looked over to the right and saw that it wasn't a restaurant parking lot. He was turning into the parking lot for the Days Inn. I watched as Brad went into the office and got a key and I watched as he and Alice went into room 116 and I was still watching when the two of the came out of the room two hours later.

There were tears in my eyes as I drove home. Anger, hurt, humiliation and rage – I suffered a little of each as my mind tried to cope with the betrayal. I was outside again at five when he and Alice came out together and drove back to the Days Inn and went into room 116. They hadn't even given up the room.

I'd had all day to think about it and as I drove home, I made up my mind. My revenge would be to let Brad support me while I cut back on the amount of sex I gave him as I looked for lovers of my own. I would never refuse Brad sex, but I would never again be the one to initiate it. As I sat at my kitchen table and sipped a glass of white wine I thought about what I was going to do. I was going to take on a lover (or lovers) and as long as I was going to do it, I wanted one who could fuck my brains out as often as we could get together. He would need to be in good shape and have plenty of stamina. What better place to look than at a gym. While I shopped for my lover, maybe I could get rid of the extra ten pounds that I thought I was carrying.

*****

I was waiting at the door to the gym at five with Bonnie and Debbie, two of the other regulars, when she walked up and said "Good morning."

"Good morning to you. Decide to do it early?"

"Need to get it done before I go to work. Can't do it during the day and I have too much going on in the evenings so here I am. Besides, if I come in when you do, you can keep an eye on me and make sure I don't do something dumb and maybe hurt myself."

Oh, I would most definitely keep an eye on her I thought to myself. I saw Bonnie and Debbie look at each other and smile when Minnie said that. I had tried to hit on both of them at one time or another and with no luck. Debbie had almost been tempted, but she was engaged and Bonnie was happily married. I had already noticed the absence of rings on Minnie's ring finger, but that might not mean anything. She might have taken them off to exercise. I'd just have to play it by ear.

Linda unlocked the door at five on the dot and Minnie and I headed for the circuit room while Bonnie and Debbie headed for the lap pool. I helped Minnie get started on machine number one – the leg press – and then I went to the free weight room and got a twenty-five pound weight, went to the rack and did fifty crunches. By the time I was done, Minnie was on the second machine in the circuit – the chest press. I watched her for a minute or so and then moved to the leg press.

As I worked out, I watched Minnie and the more I watched, the more certain I was that I was going to take a shot at her and I started thinking of how to make my move. First, I figured that I'd better give it a couple of days to develop some sort of rapport, but then I thought that she might not come back. She wouldn't be the first one to start an exercise program, go once or twice, and then decide that staying in bed for that extra hour of sleep was more inviting. If I was going to go for it it had better be now. Doing the crunches had put me behind and it would be necessary for me to finish up when Minnie did so I skipped the seated leg curl and only did one set of thirty reps on the shoulder press and then I grabbed a quick shower.

I was leaning on the front counter leafing through some brochures when Minnie came out of the women's locker room. As she came toward me, I turned and faced her.

"Got time for a cup of coffee?"

She looked at her watch and then said, "Since I showered here and only need to dress for work when I get home I guess I have time. The juice bar here?"

"No. Too many people will stop to say hi. How about the IHOP on the corner?"

"That will work."

When she settled on the seat across from me, I said, "So how do you feel after your first full workout?"

"Not bad. My legs are okay, but my arms feel like they are made out of lead."

"Your arms just aren't used to it. Back off to a lighter weight for the next couple of workouts and then gradually increase it when you get used to exercising."

"And that will take what, about five or six years?"

"Oh come on now, it won't be that bad. Didn't you say that you had a treadmill and a Stairmaster at home?"

"Yeah, but I don't think I mentioned that they also make me ache."

As she sipped her coffee, I made a point of looking at my watch and then I said:

"I know you will need to leave soon to get ready for work and I know that I don't have much time, so I'll just have to jump in with both feet. I would like to get to know you better. Would you like to have dinner with me tonight?"

"I would like that, but I don't know if I can make it tonight. Why don't you give me a number where I can reach you and as soon as I get to work and check my calendar I'll give you a call."

We finished our coffee and she got up to leave. I admired her tight looking ass as she walked toward the front door. If I had any kind of luck at all I would find out just how tight it was.

*****

I could feel his eyes on my ass as I headed for the door. I wasn't sure, but I thought that Brad would be "working late" that night and I would call him as soon as I got to work and find out. If he was going to be working late, I would have dinner with Rob. Dinner and just maybe something else. It would depend on Rob. If he was a fast worker, he could get lucky. I didn't really want to behave like a slut so I wouldn't be making any moves, but I had decided on Rob as my revenge lover and the sooner we got to it the better I would like it.

Brad was already gone when I got home so on the off chance that I would be having dinner with Rob I selected a bra and panty set that I had purchased at Victoria's Secret to tantalize Brad but which he would now never see and then I pulled on a dress that showed my legs to their best advantage. I put my sexiest heels in a tote bag. I'd put them on after work if I was going to meet Rob. For work I chose a pair of flats.

Ten minutes after getting to work I was on the phone to Brad. "I don't remember honey. Did you say you were going to be working late tonight?"

"Yes, I will be. Why?"

"If you are going to be late, I'm going to do some shopping. I saw something that I want to try on."

"Something sexy?"

"Oh yes, very sexy. I just hope that it fits."

I hung up on Brad and called Rob and told him I was free that evening if he still wanted to take me to dinner and got a yes. I spent the day thinking about what I was planning on doing and by quitting time I had totally changed my attitude. Where I had planned on not making any moves and would just wait for Rob to make them, I had now decided not to pussyfoot around. I intended to cuckold Brad and so I should just get on with it.

Rob was waiting for me in the lobby when I got off work and as I walked toward him he softly whistled and said:

"Wow! What a difference from when you are in workout clothes."

"You like?" I said as I spun around in front of him in my sexy high heels."

"Oh yeah. You are looking good. No, make that you look fantastic."

"Good enough to eat?"

"What?"

"Let's stop playing games sweetie. I know what you want and I want it too. You want to waste time having dinner or would you rather get right to the desert?"

"When you put it that way the decision is simple. My apartment is thirty minutes from here and I don't want to waste thirty minutes. There is a hotel at the end of this block. We can be in a room in ten."

Actually, it was fifteen, but who was counting.

Rob was a marvelous lover and he gave me several orgasms before I had to finally put a stop to the evening.

"I need to get going lover. I need to beat my husband home."

I saw the look that crossed his face and said, "Yes sweetie, I'm married, but I won't let it get in the way of our having fun. I assume you would like to do this again?"

"Silly question. When?"

"It can only be on the nights that he works late or is out of town. How do you feel about being on call?"

"It works for me."

"There is also the fact that this hotel is only one block from where I work and I can take long lunches."

"Would tomorrow be a long lunch day?"

"Absolutely. My lobby at twelve?"

"No. Here as soon as you can get here. I'll already have the room when you get here. That will give us just a tad more time."

"I like a man who thinks ahead."

I kissed him and headed for home.

*****

As she left the hotel room, I wondered what kind of dim bulb she was married to that he couldn't keep her at home. She was intelligent, witty, easy to talk with, drop dead gorgeous and an absolute tiger in bed. In fact, she had so much going for her that if she wasn't married, I'd consider going after her with the idea of making it a permanent arrangement and that was saying something considering I'd promised myself never again after the five year disaster that my marriage had been. Those five years with Annabelle had me saying that I'd kill myself before I'd ever get into a long term relationship again.

Then along comes something like Minnie. And she's married. Well, no one ever said that life would be fair. I'd played with married ladies before and I knew that there was one thing you could count on and that was that it wouldn't last. Maybe four or five months if you were lucky. But then four or five months with something as nice as Minnie was better than no Minnie at all and who knows, she just might be the one who would go longer. One could only hope.

*****

I beat Brad home and was in bed, freshly showered, and douched when he got there. I wasn't all that keen on having sex with him, knowing that I was going to be getting Alice's leftovers. I did want to give him Rob's. And who knows, I might luck out and have the night be one of the ones when he really did work late.

I was lying on the bed naked. I was propped up on a pillow and reading Stephen Frey's "Forced Out" when Brad walked into the room. I put the book down and spread my legs and then said:

"See anything you might like?"

He just grinned and started undressing.

I almost had an orgasm when I pushed his head down so he could eat my pussy, and I did have an orgasm thinking about Rob as Brad fucked me. It was a very satisfying evening for me.

*****

I was at the gym door talking with Bonnie and waiting for Linda to unlock the door when Minnie got there. The three of us made general conversation until Linda opened up. We checked in at the counter and got our towels and as Bonnie headed for the stairs Minnie leaned over and whispered in my ear:

"Don't wear yourself out this morning lover. You will need your strength come lunch time."

"No fair" a voice from behind us said, "I saw him first and I've known him longer."

We turned and saw Debbie standing there. Minnie looked at Debbie and then back at me and said:

"Oops."

I smiled at Minnie and said, "Ignore her. I gave her a chance and she shot me down."

"What did you expect?" Debbie said, "You hadn't shaved in a week and what girl wants to put up with a hairy bear."

"That's not what you told me at the time. You told me that your fiancée wouldn't like it."

"Well yeah, that too."

The girls headed for their locker room and I headed for the men's locker room. I put my work clothes in the locker and then headed for the treadmill. I put in twenty minutes at five miles an hour to get my heart rate up and then moved to the circuit room. Minnie was in the free weights room with Bonnie and Debbie and they were showing her some exercises she could do using barbells. I had moved through six of the circuit machines before she came into the circuit room. I finished my workout before she was halfway through the circuit so I walked over to the shoulder press where she was in the middle of her set. I waited until she did the last repetition and then said:

"Noon? For sure?"

"You can bet on it."

"I'll already have the room and I'll be waiting in the lobby for you."

"Did you take your vitamins this morning?"

"No."

"Better get some. I plan to be very active and I would like it if you could at least try to keep up."

"All I can promise is that I will do my best."

The hours seemed to drag along at work. The more I thought of meeting Minnie for a long lunch hour the slower time seemed to go. Finally, after a couple of years, it was eleven forty-five. As I left the office, I told the receptionist that I would be having a long lunch with a client if anyone came asking about me. I was sitting in the hotel lobby, room key in my pocket, when I saw Minnie come in the front door. I got up and walked to the elevator, pushed the button and waited for the door to open. Minnie walked up and we stood there not talking or acknowledging each other. There wasn't any way that anyone watching would have known that we were together.

The car arrived, the door opened and the two of us walked inside. As soon as the door was fully closed, we were in a clinch. I had my hand in her blouse and she was pulling my zipper down. When the door opened on three, we raced for room 306. Once inside it was a race to see who could get their clothes off first. Minnie won because she cheated. She didn't take off her nylons, garter belt or heels.

Minnie almost didn't leave me enough strength to go back to work. I began to wonder if I even needed to go to the gym with the workouts she was giving me.

*****

As I rode the elevator down from the third floor I thought back over the day. It had been most informative. It started when I was in the locker room with Bonnie and Debbie. As I was putting my stuff in my locker Bonnie said:

"Is Rob your first revenge fuck?"

"I beg your pardon?"

"I asked if Rob is your first revenge fuck."

"I have no idea what you are talking about."

"You don't recognize us? You really have no idea of who we are?"

"I don't believe I've ever seen either one of you before I started coming here."

"Well, I guess we did look a lot different in heels and evening dresses but I thought for sure that you would have recognized our voices. Tell me, does this sound familiar? "Do you think she suspects that he is taking Alice to the motel for long lunches?"

She saw from the look on my face that I finally knew what she was talking about.

"Debbie and I saw you go into the coat room. You were meant to hear what we said. I'm betting that you checked it out and found out that it was true. Suddenly you are here working out and Rob has that "well fucked" look on his face so the question is, is he your first revenge fuck?"

I had looked from one to the other, shrugged and then said, "Yes he is."

I had looked at both of them again and then had asked, "You disliked Brad that much that you had to make sure that I knew what he was doing?"

"It wasn't as much disliking Brad as hating Alice" Bonnie said, "We both despise her. And to be honest about it, I'm not too keen on Brad either. I can't stand a cheater. My ex cheated on me and it destroyed our family. Our kids are still having trouble getting over our divorce."

"I have the same basic problem" Debbie said. "My fiancée is an ex-fiancée because I caught him playing stink finger with one of my now ex-girlfriends."

I remembered the conversation I'd overheard and asked them if it was true that Brad had hit on them and they both said that he had. Then they told me that he had hit on almost every woman in the office – married and single – and he had scored with at least three of them in addition to Alice. Then Debbie hit me with a question that I didn't have an answer for.

"Is Rob going to be the first? Are you going to try other lovers?"

"Why do you want to know that?"

"I don't know; just curious."

"Oh bullshit" Bonnie said. "The truth is that she has had her eye on Rob since she dumped her fiancée. What she wants to know is are you keeping him or are you going to move on to someone else so she can go after Rob."

I'd had to think about that for a couple of seconds before I admitted that I didn't really know what I was going to do. I explained that I had gone after Rob, so I would have something to throw into Brad's face and that I had never considered going after lovers plural. It gave me something to think about.

*****

I looked down at her as she slept soundly next to me. I noticed what I thought was a slight smile on her face and I hoped that it was because of me. God knows I'd worked hard at trying to make sure that she enjoyed what we were doing. I still marveled at the stupidity of her husband. That he didn't do all in his power to keep her at home with him just absolutely astounded me. The more time I spent with her the more I wished that she wasn't married.

The last seven months had been magic for me. Minnie had made me change my mind about never getting into another long term relationship. She had made me want to make her mine forever. Not that I could tell her that. She had done nothing that would lead me to believe that what we had was anything more than a sexual interlude that would some day end and I was careful not to say or do anything that would bring that day closer. I very much wanted to hold onto what I had, long lunches at two and sometimes three times a week, entire nights when her husband was out of town on business, and the occasional quickie after our morning workouts at the gym. I just could not get enough of her. If I couldn't have her full time I hoped that I could at least have her part-time for the next twenty or thirty years.

*****

I woke him with a blow job and when he was up (both awake AND erect) I moved over him and used my right hand to guide him into me. It was a simply marvelous way to start the day. As we showered together, I had to keep pushing his hands away or we would have ended up back on the bed and I would have ended up being late for work. I wanted to end up back on the bed. I was still hot from what had happened when Brad made his nightly 'check-in' phone call. Rob was doing me doggie when the call came and he wouldn't pull out and let me take the call.

I scooted across the bed to the phone with Rob coming along behind me. We were like two dogs in heat tied together by the knot in the dog's cock. I answered the call and then talked with Brad while Rob kept slowly fucking me. I was so hot that my pussy still tingled, as I thought about it eight hours later. After I hung up, I tried to berate Rob for his actions, but he just smiled and said:

"Bitch all you want lover, but you loved it."

And I had. Oh God had I ever. We went to the gym for our morning workout and then we stopped and had breakfast at the IHOP. Over French toast I asked:

"Long lunch today or did you get enough last night?"

"You know the answer to that one."

"Oh yeah? And what would that be?"

"I can never get enough of you."

"Long lunch it is then. Take your vitamins."

On the way from IHOP to work, I wondered just how long I was going to keep seeing Rob before having my confrontation with my "loving husband." My original plan was to have a short affair, confront Brad about his affair with Alice, throw mine with Rob in his face and then ask him if he wanted to stop the running around and try to make the marriage work. That was before finding out from Debbie and Bonnie about his other affairs.

Armed with what Debbie and Bonnie told me, I had done some

discrete investigating and had found out that Brad had three short affairs with girls who worked at Chambers Brothers after he had married me and before he had taken his current job. The question I had been asking myself for months, was did I want to try and make the marriage work? But more and more, I found myself thinking that the answer to that question was "No, not really."

I was having a blast giving Brad well used pussy. I made sure that I had sex with Brad after having made love to Rob. It was rarely 'right after' but always on the same day. I was always showered and douched so he wouldn't ever suspect. But except for when he went out of town, I always gave myself to Brad within hours of when Rob pulled out of me.

I was enjoying the hell out of cuckolding my husband.

And, I suddenly realized, I didn't want to give up Rob.

Now what do I do?

*****

I had the room key in my hand when I saw her coming in the front entrance. Between the time we'd had breakfast at the IHOP and the time I checked in and got the room key I'd had a complete change of heart. I was killing myself – at least mentally – by continuing my affair with Minnie. I had to admit to myself that I was hopelessly in love with her and not being able to have her full time was really messing me up. My work was suffering because Minnie was always on my mind. When I wasn't with her, I was always look forward to when it would be.

I had no life when I wasn't with her. I'd sit in my apartment and stare at the walls and think about her and count the minutes until it was time to hit the gym in the morning and see her again. We had talked and I knew why she was seeing me and she showed no interest in ever leaving her husband.

I couldn't continue on treating her as only part time in my life. For my own good, I needed to end it. I would even have to change gyms, so I wouldn't have to suffer seeing her. As I watched her walk toward the elevator where I was waiting, I knew that it would be a hard thing to do, but I also knew that I had to do it.

*****

Brad came into the bedroom with a towel wrapped around his waist and still dripping from his shower. As I slipped my heels on, I asked him what time he would be home for dinner and when he said he would be working late again, something in my mind snapped. As I picked up my purse from the dresser, I said:

"Why don't you just go ahead and spend the night with Alice instead of trying to hurry home, that way I can spend the night at Rob's place instead of rushing home and I can be here when you get here."

"What the hell are you saying?"

"You know well what I'm saying Brad, but not to worry sweetie; no need for a divorce. You just see Alice or whomever when you get the urge and don't worry about me, Rob will keep me occupied."

I headed for the front door and he yelled, "Just a god damned minute Minerva. Are you telling me that you are cheating on me with a guy named Rob? Who the fuck is Rob?"

"He's the guy I took up with when I found out about Alice, Mary, Wendy, Sally (the names Bonnie and Debbie had given me), Doris, Beverly and Charlotte (the girls who worked at Chambers Brothers). At least, I only took one instead of a herd."

"What the fuck does that have to do with anything? I'm a man and all men play on the side. You are my wife and you are supposed to keep yourself for me."

That statement caught me by surprise and the ridiculousness of it made me laugh.

"This is no laughing matter Minerva. There is no way I am going to have a whore for a wife."

I was still laughing as I left the house. On the drive to work, I thought back over the last twenty-four hours. I met Rob at the motel and we made mad, passionate love. As we were leaving, Rob told me that it was our last time. He told me how he felt and that he just couldn't go on. I wasn't prepared for that. Somehow I had thought that he would always be there.

I spent the rest of the day at work in a funky mood and really wasn't sure why. Last night, I had cheered up some as I fed Brad Rob's leftovers, but when we were done I had trouble sleeping. In the morning, I had gone to the gym, but Rob wasn't there. I went through my workout and then had gone home to hear Brad's ridiculous statement that cheating was okay for him because he was a man. The thought of that got me laughing again.

*****

Work sucked. All I could think about was Minnie and the fact that I would never see her again. The fact that my cell phone went off every ten minutes and the screen showed that the caller was Minnie didn't help any.

I managed to get through the morning and just before lunch, my secretary stuck her head in the door and told me that my eleven-thirty appointment was in the outer office. I checked my calendar, but didn't see an appointment for that morning. It wouldn't be the first time that something got screwed up so I got up and went to the outer office. Minnie was standing there. I didn't know what to say so I just said,

"Good morning. Come on into the office."

I stood aside to let her walk in and then I followed and closed the door behind me. She turned to face me and said:

"I was afraid that you might forget our lunch date so I thought I would drop by and we could go together."

I started to say something, but Minnie held up her hand to stop me.

"I heard what you said yesterday Rob, but you are my friend and friends need to stick together during rough times. I'm going to need someone to hold my hand, while I go through a messy divorce and then maybe comfort me when it is over. Can I count on you to be there for me?"

End of the 1ˢᵗ Story

-
-
-
-
-
-
-

The Layoff

-
-
-
-
-
-
-

The story starts in early June of 2002. My boss called me into his office and told me that he was going to have to file for bankruptcy and then he told me not to worry, that my final paycheck would be covered and then he asked me to stay with him until the day that he actually had to close the doors. He had been good to me during the five years I'd been with him, so I said I'd stay.

Over the coming weeks I worked with vendors who came in and picked up merchandise and credited back to Dale's account. Two days before the day that Dale had designated as the final day one of his largest competitors came in and introduced himself to me and then asked me what I planned on doing when Dale closed his doors. I admitted that I hadn't looked that far ahead and then he asked me if I would consider coming to work for him.

"Doing what?"

"The same thing that you did here. I'm expanding and I need a good combo service manager and mechanic, and most of your customers have a very good opinion of you."

"I'm not sure that it would be a good move for me. Dale had a thriving business here and he went under. You're in the same business, so how can I believe that you won't go down too. It could be a case of jumping from the frying pan into the fire."

"It wasn't the core business that killed Dale. It was all the different areas he tried to move into. He had to borrow money to expand and when the expansion didn't make money, he couldn't pay his debts. What is Dale paying you?"

I told him and he told me that he would pay me a dollar an hour more to start and then review it in ninety days. I had nothing else on the line, so I figured why not? If it didn't work out I'd have had to look for a job anyway when Dale closed. I'd just be putting off the job search. I told him okay.

"When is your last day here?"

"We close the door on the sixteenth."

"I'll see you on the seventeenth, okay?"

We shook on it and he went out, got in his car and drove off. That was the start of my relationship with Paul Notting.

Two days later, Dale handed me my final paycheck and thanked me for sticking with him. I looked at the check and saw that it was for five hundred more than I had coming and Dale said:

"That would have been your Christmas bonus if we could have made it that far."

We shook hands and wished each other luck.

*****

The next day, I walked into Paul's place of business and the first thing I saw when I came through the door was a breath taking raven haired beauty sitting at a desk. My cock went instantly to full hard, but before I could say anything to the woman, Paul came in and said:

"Oh good, you're here. Mellissa this is Rob; Rob this is my wife Mellissa. Rob is our new service manager. Take care of his paperwork will you? I've got to run over to Clarksville and see Greening" then he was gone.

Mellissa looked up at me and smiled. "You look disappointed" she said.

"I am. I most definitely am."

"Well take heart. Paul has been known to piss me off so bad that

I have to do things to get even with him."

"What kinds of things?"

"No telling. It is never the same thing twice."

That conversation set the tone of my relationship with Mellissa. Did you ever know a woman who could make your dick and your tongue hard with just the sound of her voice? Just imagine what her five foot six one, hundred and twenty pound body, arranged as 36 x 22 x 35 did to me, if just her voice could crank me.

And Mellissa was evil!

Mellissa knew the effect that she had on me and she exploited it. She teased me and flirted with me shamelessly. Never when Paul was around, but if he wasn't there and there were no customers around, she would torture me. She would tell me how horny she was and how she wished that Paul was there so they could catch a quickie on his desk.

She wore skirts and dresses to work and would call me into the office on some pretext or other and she would be sitting in her chair with the hems pulled up so I could see just a touch of panty. Once I saw a touch of pussy hair because she wasn't wearing any panties, It got to where I both looked forward to going to work and dreaded going to work.

*****

This went on for three years and for three years, I behaved myself. It was hard, but I wasn't the kind of guy who messed around with some other guy's woman, so I both enjoyed it and suffered in silence.

One day, and I remember it well – it was the seventeenth of July, my third anniversary with the company – I came to work and Paul called me into his office and told me that Mellissa and I had to hold down the fort that day. Out in the shop Mark was on vacation, and Bill had called in sick.

"I have to run over to Clarksville and I'm taking Saul with me."

"No problem" I said, "Mellissa and I can handle it."

Around ten, Mellissa paged me on the inter-com. "Rob, can you come up to the office please?"

I wiped my hands on a rag and went up to see what she wanted. Mellissa was wearing a blouse and a skirt that day, along with nylons and heels and I was instantly as hard as a steel bar.

"You rang?"

"Yes Rob; I need you to keep an eye out and let me know if anyone is coming. I need to make an adjustment."

She started unbuttoning her blouse. I quickly stepped to the door and turned the deadbolt. Mellissa didn't see me do it because she was looking down at her blouse. At the time, the only significance of locking the door was that I knew that Mellissa was going to tease me again and I didn't want to have to keep one eye on the door and have only one eye on Mellissa. I thought I was only going to get a quick view of her bra covered tits, but Mellissa took off her blouse and then unhooked and removed her bra.

Her tits were magnificent! They looked like the tips of torpedoes or missiles; cone shaped and firm. I was struck dumb. I was frozen to the spot and Mellissa said:

"I must not have been paying attention when I bought this bra. It is a size too small and it was killing me."

She reached up and rolled her nipples between her fingers. "God, I'm horny. Why is Paul always gone when I really need him?"

She put her blouse back on and went to walk by me. As she went by, she reached down and rubbed my hard cock and said:

"You should really find someone to take care of that for you."

I lost it! I lost it totally! Three years of frustration and want exploded out of me and without any thought of what I was doing I grabbed Mellissa and spun her around and sat her down on her desk. My hands were up her skirt and I was tossing her panties on the floor before she even realized what was happening. I pulled her up off the desk, spun her around and pushed her down until her tits were pressing into the desk top. In less time than it would take to say "You fucking prick-tease" I had my swollen cock out and pressing against her cunt, as she started to say:

"What the hell do you think you are doing" but only got as far as "you think…" before I drove into her.

She was wet. She was soaking wet. Her teasing must have turned her on as much as it made me hard. She grunted as I drove into her. Three thrusts and I was all the way in her and Mellissa was moaning:

"You can't… we can't… you bastard… not right… you bastard; you bastard, BASTARD, YOU FUCKING BASTARD!!!"

But a funny thing was taking place. As she moaned and called me names, she was pushing back at my invading cock. I stopped thrusting and stood still as Mellissa moved back and forth fucking herself on my dick. She rammed herself back at me as she cried:

"You miserable asshole, bastard, low life cocksucker" and then she screamed, "Why the fuck did you stop!!?? Fuck me, damn you, fuck me!!"

I started pounding into her and the harder I fucked her the louder her cries, but the cries changed to:

"YES, YES, YES, YES, MAKE ME CUM DAMN YOU, FUCK ME, MAKE ME CUM!"

I was pounding her hard and sweating bullets when she screamed out:

"Oh yes, oh fuck, oh fuck yes!" and her body shook like a dog trying to shit peach pits. I was close and I kept slamming into her and just as I got my nut, she screamed "Oh shit!" and her body shook again. I held myself in her until I started to go soft and she started saying:

"Get off of me goddamn it; get the fuck off of me!"

I pulled out of her, said to myself, "Fuck it! In for a penny, in for a pound" and I grabbed her, turned her to face me and then pushed her to her knees in front of me.

"Clean it bitch!"

As I pushed my cock at her face I expected her to look up at me and say "Fuck you asshole" but she opened her mouth and went to work cleaning our combined juices off of me. Her mouth work had predictable results and I lifted her up, sat her on the desk and pushed her until she was lying on her back. She looked up at me with an expressionless face and slowly, but very deliberately, opened her legs. I stepped between them and drove my cock into her soaking cunt. Her legs came up and clamped me and she said:

"Fuck me asshole; fuck me!"

The second fuck was a silent fuck as she stared up at me and held me between her legs as her hands clutched my ass and pulled me to her. For several minutes we looked into each other's eyes, as I fucked her as hard as I could. Then she started to moan:

"Oh yes, that's it, like that, oh yes, make me cum, make me cum, make m... OH SHIT!" and her body shook again.

Not many seconds later, I sent my sperm rocketing into her. I drained and slowly pulled out of her. She looked up at me and said:

"I'm not cleaning it off this time. We both know what will happen if I do and we do have to get some work done around here today."

I grabbed the hem of her skirt and wiped myself off and then I turned and went back to the shop leaving her lying on the desk.

Mellissa and I avoided each other for the rest of the day.

At home that night, I looked at myself in the mirror and had the thought "So much for being the kind of guy who doesn't mess with another guy's woman." But was it really my fault? Didn't Mellissa do everything but flat out ask me to fuck her? Did she want it? Was she hoping for it? Or was she just being her evil teasing self? All she had to do was go into the bathroom to take care of her bra problem. True, she didn't fight me off, but she didn't come right out and say "Do me" either. What she did do was be submissive to me. Was that it? Did she need to be told what to do? Did she need to believe that she was being made to do it? I spent a fairly sleepless night wondering what was going to happen at work the next day.

*****

Nothing happened at work the next day. Mellissa acted as if nothing untoward had happened and Paul acted like he had no idea of what Mellissa and I had done. Had Mellissa told him? Was he one of those guys who lets his wife go out and play? Was he the kind who liked to hear her tell about what she had done and with who? I had no way of knowing and so I stayed away from the office. It wasn't my fault! She asked for it! Maybe not with words, but her actions had screamed out "Fuck me!" and so I had.

Nevertheless, I stayed in the shop and didn't go up to the front office. I avoided Mellissa and it seemed that she was doing her best to avoid me. The few times I had to go up to the office Mellissa behaved. There was none of the flirting that had once been a daily staple of our relationship. This is not to say that I totally ignored Mellissa. I could not keep from looking at the sexy bitch, but it was strictly a case of look, but don't touch and don't even talk unless business forced me to.

This state of affairs went on for the next three weeks. One Thursday morning, Paul told me he had to go over to Waltersburg and would be gone overnight.

"I may not be back before quitting time tomorrow, so it will be up to you to lock the place up for the weekend."

"No problem."

"Stan Witczak asked if he could borrow the trailer so if he stops by let him have it."

"Will do."

I was always the last one out of the shop at night and I made the rounds checking windows, doors and lights. I made sure the air compressor was shut off and then I went to the service desk and started the procedure for shutting down the computer. While I was doing that, I saw Mellissa come out of the office and head for me and when I turned to her to see what she wanted or needed she slapped me hard across the face and snarled at me:

"You miserable bastard! How could you do to me what you did to me and then ignore me?"

She went to slap me again and I caught her wrist and said, "Bullshit! If you wanted any attention from me, you would have given me some indication."

"Like what?"

"Like everything you did that caused the last time to happen. For three years, you teased the ass off of me for the last three weeks. Nothing, but since it is obvious to me now that you want more of what you got the last time, let's get to it."

I put my hands on her shoulders and pushed her down on her knees.

"What the hell are you doing?"

"You know damn well, so get to it."

She looked up at me and snarled "Bastard!" but as she said it, she was reaching for my zipper. I let her suck on me until I was ready to cum and then I grabbed her head and fucked her face until I came. I shot into her mouth and she tried to jerk back, but I held her head and she was forced to swallow. When my cock started to go soft I released her head and she pulled back and screamed at me,

"You miserable cock sucking bastard; I don't swallow."

"You do when it is my cock in your mouth and don't you ever forget it. Now get your damned panties off and get your ass up there on the desk."

I may not be the smartest guy in the world, but I am not totally stupid either. The way Mellissa had behaved our first time and the way she had behaved when I had just then pushed her to her knees told me that Mellissa wanted or felt the need to be dominated. She confirmed it.

"Who the hell are you to be ordering me around?"

"I am your fucking owner. Any time you are silly enough to let yourself be alone with me, I own you and you will do whatever the hell I tell you do. Now get your panties off and get on that desk."

She gave me a nasty look, but she took off her panties and got up on the desk.

"You know what to do now," I said and she spread her legs wide and then I surprised her. She expected me to step forward and take her, but I went to my knees and went to work on her pussy with my mouth. In less than a minute she was moaning, had her fingers in my hair and was pulling me to her. I worked on her until I was hard again and then I pulled her up, bent her over the desk and fucked her. She was very vocal. Among the things I heard were:

"Fuck me, fuck me hard." "Make me cum damn you, make me cum." "Faster damn it, harder. If you are going to fuck me then make it harder."

She came twice – at least I think she did – and then I shot my wad, pulled out and said:

"You know what to do."

She gave me a nasty look, but without a word she got down and cleaned my cock with her mouth. When she finally stood up I told her to go on home and leave her front door unlocked.

"When I get there I want you naked, on your bed and with your legs spread waiting for me."

"I'm not fucking you in my house and on my bed."

"I'll fuck you in the middle of the street in front of this building if I want to. I'm not asking you shit you teasing bitch; I'm telling you. Get your ass home and get ready for me."

She gave me a long hard look and then turned and left.

*****

I locked up and headed out. I stopped at a store and picked up a few things and then I headed for Mellissa's house. As I drove I thought about the situation. I didn't go looking for it. I never would have gone looking for it, but I had had it handed to me on a platter and wouldn't I have been criminally stupid not to take advantage of it? I was under no illusions. I doubted that I was anything to Mellissa but an interlude, but she was the sexiest woman I had ever known and it wasn't likely that I would ever get another chance at one like her so I had to go for it.

I didn't know how long the domination thing would last and in fact, it might already be over. I'd know when I got to the house. If the door was locked instead of open I'd know that it was over.

The domination thing isn't about the whips, chains and ball gags kind. I believed that it was something that Mellissa was doing so she could lay in bed next to her husband and say to herself:

"I'm not really cheating. I don't want to do it, but he is making me. I can't stop him. I've tried, but I can't stop him" or some kind of shit like that. Whatever, I decided that I was going to take as much of Mellissa as she would let me have. I had no doubt that if she decided to end it, she would do it firmly.

Surprise, surprise. The front door was not only not locked, but was even open just a crack when I got there. When I walked into the bedroom I found her just as I'd told her to be. She looked at me and asked:

"What's in the bag?"

"Astroglide."

"What do you need that for?"

"It will make things easier when I push my cock in your ass."

"I don't do that."

"You don't do that with anyone else, maybe, but you will do it with me."

"I don't wa…"

"When are you going to wake up to the fact that what you want or don't want doesn't mean shit to me? When you are with me what I want is all that counts."

I tossed her the bag and she caught it and set it on the bed next to her and then she watched me while I stripped off my clothes. I wondered what she was thinking because it would be the first time she saw me with my clothes off. She didn't burst out laughing or get a look of disgust on her face so I took that as a good sign.

I moved onto the bed next to her and then spun around and moved over her into a 'sixty-nine' and said, "You know what to do." As I buried my face in her pussy I felt her twist a bit under me and then I felt her hot mouth close around my cock. After several minutes I moved, pulled out of her mouth, pulled her up and maneuvered her onto her hands and knees. As I pushed into her, she gasped and moaned.

"Oh yes, oh fuck yes." As I felt her push back at me she moaned, "This isn't right damn you." I gripped her hips and drove myself into her. "Not right, not right, you bastard… oh God, oh God fuck me, damn you, fuck me."

I picked up the pace and was pounding her hard when the bedside phone rang. "Shit! Not now," she cried, "Not now' and she tried to pull away from me to get to the phone. I held her and kept fucking her.

"Let me go. Damn you Rob, let me go."

"No. You're busy right now."

"I have to answer it. It's Paul."

"So what?"

"He's my husband damn it; I have to take his call."

"He's nobody. He's just someone you know when you are with me. He is of no consequence when you are with me. When we are alone together, you are mine. I own you."

"What am I going to tell him when he asks why I didn't answer the phone?"

"Tell him you were busy fucking me or tell him some lie. Up to you or you can answer and talk to him while I'm still fucking you. Makes no mind to me."

The phone stopped ringing and she cried, "You bastard! You worthless bastard!"

"Worthless? Worthless?"

I stopped fucking her and started to pull back.

"What are you doing?"

"I'm worthless right? You shouldn't be wasting your time with a worthless bastard."

"God damn you Rob! Don't you dare stop now. Fuck me Rob; please don't stop fucking me."

"Are you sure?"

"Damn you Rob, fuck me!"

I shoved back into as hard as I could and she grunted and then cried, "Oh yes! Yes yes yes yes!! Harder, fuck me harder."

I know that she had orgasms, but I wasn't paying any attention. I concentrated on reaching my own and when I got it, I felt like I was shooting into her with the force of a fire hose. I shot so hard, I half expected to see the cum squirt out of her mouth. I pulled out and Mellissa fell to the bed. I stayed on my knees and said:

"You know what to do now."

She turned onto her back and looked up at me and I saw on her face that she was going to refuse.

"Do it now!" I snarled, "Or I'll sit on the edge of the bed with my hand on the phone and wait for your hubby to call back. What do you think his reaction will be to my answering the phone?" I looked at my watch and said, "You have sixty seconds. After that I won't let you do it and I'll sit here with my hand on the phone if it takes until tomorrow."

I looked at the second hand on my watch and after forty seconds Mellissa moved and her mouth started working on my cock. When she was done, she fell back on the bed and looked up at me as if to say:

"Okay, what's next?"

Before I could say anything, the phone rang and Mellissa rolled over on her stomach and answered it. It was Paul. She lied and told him that she was on the toilet when he called earlier and then they talked about the things married couples talk about while I knelt there and looked at Mellissa's perfect heart shaped ass.

I smiled and moved and straddled her legs as I reached for the bag I'd tossed to her earlier. I took the Astroglide out of the bag and coated the fingers of my right hand. Mellissa tensed when she felt my fingers slide between her ass cheeks and then she suddenly realized what I intended to do. She tried to squirm away from me, but I had her legs pinned. She couldn't very well turn and tell me to stop while she was on the phone with Paul now could she?

I heard a slight gasp as my first finger entered her ass and then I heard her tell Paul that it was nothing. She was drinking a Coke with ice and an ice cube has slipped out of the glass and fallen on her breast. Next she had to explain that she was sitting in bed naked reading and that's why the gasp when the ice cube fell onto her naked breast. Then she had to explain that she was sitting in bed naked because she was horny and playing with herself.

Just about the time I worked a second finger into her butt hole, she lost it and hollered through the phone:

"Because I'm horny as hell and I need a cock and you aren't here. What the fuck is with all the fucking questions?"

"No! I'm not in the mood anymore."

I poured some Astroglide between the crack of her ass and worked a third finger into her while she apologized for blowing up at him and then there was the usual "I miss you and I wish you were here" followed by "Hurry home baby, I need you" just before she hung up. As soon as the handset was in the cradle she yelled:

"What the fuck are you doing?" as she tried to get out from under me.

I held her down and said, "I'm getting your ass ready to fuck."

"I told you I don't do that. I don't even let Paul do that."

"I already told you that I don't give a shit what you want. I own you bitch. Your mouth is mine, your cunt is mine and your ass is mine and if you never give it to Paul that's between the two of you, but I'm taking it."

I got off of her legs and pulled her up to her knees. The moment of truth came when I let go of her hips to coat my cock with Astroglide. I wasn't holding her or pinning her down and all she had to do was pull away and scurry off the bed. She didn't move. I aimed my cock at her rosebud and pushed against it. She still didn't move. I grabbed her hips and leaned into her. She gasped as I pushed into her and moaned:

"You bastard, you filthy bastard. I don't want this."

But when I took my hands off of her hips and held myself still she didn't try to pull away. I slowly fucked her tight hole and after a couple of minutes I felt her push back a little. I kept at it slow and easy as she moaned:

"Dirty, dirty, not right, disgusting, oooh God."

I pulled back until I was almost out of her and then stopped.

"No, damn it, no," she cried as she drove herself back on my cock. I smiled and went back to fucking her ass. I'd already cum so many times that night that it took me forever to bust my nut, but I finally managed to send a load to join the shit I'd already packed. I held myself in her as I drained and she kept wiggling her butt. I knew she wanted more. I knew that despite all of her protestations that she had liked a cock in her ass. She could bitch, whine and complain all she wanted, but I knew she had loved it.

She fell to the bed gasping and rolled over to look up at me and said:

"No! No fucking way am I going to clean it off with my mouth."

"You damned well would if I wanted you to, but I don't. I'm not done with you yet and I don't want to kiss you with shit on your lips."

She gave me an evil look and said, "Maybe I want to clean it after all."

I got off the bed and walked into the bathroom and was washing my cock when she came in and sat down on the toilet. She took care of her business while watching me. I looked at her and said:

"When was the last time you woke up in bed next to a man who wasn't Paul?"

"Never."

"Another first for you then."

I went back into the bedroom and laid down on my back and waited for Mellissa to come back into the room. She walked through the door and saw how I was lying and she hesitated a bit and then climbed on the bed and her hand reached for my limp cock. She looked at it, up at me and then back at the cock and then she bent her head and took it in her mouth. It took her a long time and I wasn't even sure that I could pop again, but she did coax a small load out of me and she swallowed it.

When it was soft she let it plop out of her mouth and then she looked at me and licked her lips. With one finger, she wiped up a stray drop that had escaped her mouth, licked her finger clean and then moved up to settle in beside me. "You are such an asshole," she said and then she rolled onto her side and seconds later I heard the soft easy breathing of someone asleep.

*****

In the morning I awoke with my cock in Mellissa's mouth and when I was awake enough and hard enough Mellissa handed me the Astroglide and without a word moved up onto her hands and knees.

It was easier going the second time and I didn't get any of the "dirty, filthy, disgusting" that I had gotten the night before. I did get a "yes, oh fuck yes" and a couple of "fuck me, damn you, fuck me" cries. It took me a long time and once again I wasn't sure that I would be able to cum after all that I'd done since closing time the night before. I worked at it and I sweated bullets, but I finally did cum although I'm not sure much came out but dust.

When I pulled out, she fell to the bed, rolled to the edge, and got up. She muttered "I don't understand how something so dirty and perverted can feel so good" and then she padded into the bathroom and seconds later, I heard the shower start running. I thought about joining her and scrubbing her back while she scrubbed mine, but gave it up as a bad idea. It would only lead us back to the bed and with the mornings and previous evening's activities I wasn't all that sure that I could perform. Up until then I'd given a pretty good account of myself. Best I leave it in Mellissa's mind that I was a stud.

When she came out, I went and took my shower. When I'd dressed and gone downstairs, I found her in the kitchen pouring herself a cup of coffee. She showed me where the cups were and pointed out the cream and sugar on the counter.

"I'm not much of a morning person. Breakfast is not my forte. If you need something to start your day Denny's is open."

She took a sip of her coffee and then said, "I have no idea why I allowed what happened to happen. I don't know how I let it get away from me like I did. I love my husband and he damned sure didn't deserve what I just did to him. I let you do things to me that I had never let and never will let Paul do to me and I don't know why. What I do know is that it will never happen again. Are we clear on that?"

I took a sip of my coffee and then looked her right in the eye as I said:

"Sure. Whatever you say. Your word is law. You got it! Your wish is my command. You da boss. Until the next time you come after me. I didn't start this, you did. You fucking well knew what was going to happen when you stripped in front of me and then grabbed my cock. None of it is on me. I let you tease me for over three years and never once made a move on you and we would have gone on that way another ten or twenty. You are the one who changed things, not me.

"Even after that first time I stayed away from you and again it was you who came after me so don't give me any of this "Are we clear on this" shit! You keep your hands to yourself and we don't have a problem. How about being clear on that if we are going to be clear on things?"

I put my cup down and walked out of her house.

*****

Mellissa stayed clear of me for the next two weeks and I wondered how long it would be until she made her next move. I didn't have long to wait. Friday Paul called me into the office and had me take a seat. Mellissa was at her desk, but not looking at me. Paul said:

"There isn't any easy way to do this so I guess I'd better just get it done. Business had slowed down and money has started to get tight. Mellissa has gone over and over on the books and we don't see any way we can continue on with our current payroll. You know how it goes Rob. Last in, first out, and you were my last hire. I have your final check here" and he handed it to me. "It has four weeks severance included, a week's pay for every year and part year you have been here and I of course will give you a glowing letter of reference. Again, I'm sorry. I wish it could be some other way."

I stood up and so did he and he offered me his hand and I took it and we shook. I glanced over at Mellissa and she was looking at me. No smile or smirk, but I could tell from her eyes and the set of her mouth what she was thinking.

"If there is no temptation there is no problem."

Paul was to my left and he couldn't see it when I smiled at Mellissa and winked. I turned and left the office.

The End

-
-
-
-
-
-
-
-

The Coward

-
-
-
-
-
-
-

I've finally had to admit to myself that I'm a coward. Oh, it's always been there, but I've never admitted it. As a kid, I always ran away from fights and said that discretion was the better part of valor. As an adult I walked away from things and said I was being a mature and sensible, but I can't hide it anymore. I'm a coward.

I had been out of work for almost eight months because of the faltering economy. I had papered the city with applications and resumes, but hadn't received one call. I was working three part time jobs trying to hold things together and my wife Glenda worked and between the two of us, we were just barely hanging on. Our personal life pretty much sucked because of constant arguments over money and an almost absolute lack of sex because of the hours I was working. Glenda had a nine-to-five job so she was gone from seven-thirty to around six. I worked the counter in a convenience store from three in the afternoon till eleven at night so she was asleep when I got home. I slept from the time I got home until three when I got up to go and deliver newspapers. I threw two routes so I didn't get home until after Glenda had already left for work. The only time we saw each other was on the weekend, my third part time job, flipping burgers, got in the way and when we were finally home together, I just flat couldn't stay awake.

About five months into that eight-month period I began to suspect that Glenda was having an affair, but what could I do about it? Nothing, at least not without taking a chance that a confrontation would end our marriage. So I just worked my ass off trying to hold my little world together and all the while hoping that I wouldn't lose Glenda to somebody else.

The call came out of the blue and it came from a company that I hadn't even sent a resume to. I was asked if I would be interested in coming in for an interview and when I said I would, they scheduled me for one and told me to be prepared to spend a full eight hours with them on that day. I was there at eight on the dot and was given a bunch of forms to fill out. When I handed them back to the receptionist, I was given a slip to take to Sleepy Hollow Clinic where I was given a complete physical, including an EKG, and had blood taken for God only knows how many tests. Then I was sent back to the company offices where I was given a battery of tests that took almost three hours to complete and then I was sent out to sit in the lobby and wait for the interviewer to summon me. Finally, at three in the afternoon I was told to report to Mr. Simpson in room 103 for the formal interview. Simpson introduced himself and then got right to the point.

"You are probably asking yourself why the physical and all the testing before we even talked to you. The answer is that we all ready know that you have something that we want and that you possess the experience and qualifications that we want. We have not even considered that you might say no when we make you the job offer. Our compensation and benefits package is such that only an idiot would say no. The reason for all the tests and the physical was to see if you were physically and mentally capable of fitting in here. We are what is sometimes referred to as a 'first tier' Japanese style company. What that means is that we follow the original Japanese style - employment with us is a lifetime. In rough times you may be reduced to sweeping floors, at no loss in pay I might add, or even be sent to the boss's house to wash and wax his car. But once in never out unless you quit of your own accord or you die. So you can see that we want to know everything about you that there is to know before we make you a part of our group."

He went on to explain the job, the benefits and the compensation package and he was right - only an idiot would have turned it down. Simpson asked when I could start and I told him that I needed to give two weeks notice where I was working. He frowned, "We had rather hoped that you would start immediately." I told him that I would like to, but that I had to be fair to the people I worked for. I wasn't sure, but from his facial expression I thought that I might just have passed some sort of test.

I gave my notice, worked it out and then went to work at my new job. I loved it! It was work that I had been trained to do and work that I was good at. Once I started working regular hours, decent paychecks started coming in, things got a whole lot better at home. Glenda and I began to have a sex life again, but in the back of my mind, I couldn't shake the idea that Glenda was still having her affair. She always had to work late on Thursday nights to get the payroll out, or so she said, and Tuesday night was her night to stop after work and have drinks with the girls she worked with. But she would never have sex with me on those two nights and I suspected that those were the nights when she met her lover. Again, I was afraid to confront her so I convinced myself that it would be best to leave things alone. I convinced myself that now that I had only one job and would be home all the time Glenda wouldn't need a lover and that she would eventually break off the affair.

Six months went by and things were going well and then one afternoon, Simpson called me into his office and invited Glenda and me to a party being held at the boss's house. I told Glenda to go out and buy a new dress for the party since I wanted us to make a good impression. She came home with a simple black cocktail dress that came down to mid-thigh and a pair of black pumps in the style called Come Fuck Me. A single strand of peals completed the outfit and Glenda looked stunning - sexy but elegant and I was never prouder than when we walked in the front door of the boss's house and every man there looked at Glenda and wished she were his. Simpson met us at the door, "Good, you're here. I need to talk with you in the den," and he handed Glenda off to Bob Markowitz from Accounting.

"Bob will see to getting your wife a drink and getting her introduced around. Follow me to the den."

In the den he offered me a seat and then he said, "You've been with us, what, a little over six months now? Would it be fair to say that you like your job?"

I assured him that I did.

"Have you considered the downside of working for this company?"

I told him that I wasn't aware that there was a downside.

"Oh, but there is, dear boy. Consider this - everyone knows about our policy of lifetime employment and that no one leaves us unless they quit or die. Imagine what they would think if we suddenly up and fired somebody. They would be forced to think that there was something drastically wrong with whomever we let go. They would suspect him of every evil thing under the sun and he would never work in the industry again. And of course, there is a lot of communication between our industry and other industries. Can you see what I mean?"

I told him that I saw what he meant, "But why are you telling me all of this?"

"So you will know what to expect if we were to let you go."

"I don't understand."

"It's very simple, dear boy. Several of us are going to fuck your wife tonight. It is going to happen whether you like it or not. Your choice is to not make a fuss and continue your lifetime employment with us, or you can be difficult and we will let you go and you can spend the rest of your life flipping burgers. So, there you have it. I once told you that we came after you because you had something that we wanted. That something was your wife. She has certain qualities that the company can use in our business. She is quite beautiful and she is a slut - perfect for being the company whore. Tonight will only be the first of many for her, but I'm sure she won't mind."

I sat there flabbergasted at what he was saying. Simpson saw the expression on my face and went on, "Surely you must know that Glenda isn't a faithful little wife? We learned of her through her boss who just happens to be my brother. Glenda has fucked every man who works in the office with her, and you can usually find her on her back in a motel on Thursday nights and on the back seat of a car in the bar parking lot on Tuesdays. And your Glenda is partial to gang bangs. Just the girl we need, to take care of some of our better customers. So, why don't you just run on home now, and we will call you in the morning so that you can come and collect her."

I was sitting on the couch in the living room thinking about what Simpson had told me. On my mind, I've known what Glenda was doing on Tuesdays and Thursday. Even if I wouldn't admit it to myself, but I had never even started thinking that it was anything but one lover. Gangbangs? Sweet Jesus Christ! I had wisely (and cowardly) left my meeting with Simpson and come straight home. True, I had abandoned Glenda, but why should I risk lifetime employment for a slut who had been fucking around on me? I had considered that Simpson might have been lying to me about Glenda, but then how would he have known about Tuesdays and Thursdays? No, Simpson knew what he was talking about.

I also thought about the last thing that Simpson had said to me before I left the boss's house, "We need for her to have a certain degree of respectability old boy, so do not do anything silly when you get her home. Work it out as best you can, but divorce is quite out of the question. Now be a good boy and run along. I must be getting back to the party."

Was I just going to sit back and let Simpson and the company higher ups dictate me on how I will live my life? Yes, I was. Why? Because I'm a coward. All that's left for me to do now is wait for the phone call to tell me to come and pick up Glenda.

The End

The Conversion

John was sitting in the chair watching, as I worked on Bill's cock with my mouth. He was smiling at me and slowly stroking his erection. I winked at him, took my mouth off of Bill, and got on the bed. Bill spread my legs so he could slide his hard cock into my steaming pussy for the third time that afternoon, and I moaned:

"Oh yes, oh god yes, that feels so damned good."

He lifted my legs up onto his shoulders so he could push deep into me and began fucking me hard, and I came, and came, and came. I felt him tense up and then he erupted, splashing my insides with spurt after spurt of his cum. I was astonished that he could push so much into me after already having cum in me twice.

Bill pulled out and fell to the bed beside me, but I wasn't through and I wanted more. I wanted more, much, much more. I bent my head and took his limp cock in my mouth and went to work on him. He recovered faster than I thought he would. I climbed on top of him and used my hand to guide him into me. I motioned for John to come over and join us, so he got on the bed and moved in behind me. I felt his fingers probe my ass and I hissed:

"Yes, yes, right there, put it right there."

It was a good thing that both John and Bill had already been in my ass once and had loosened it up, or John's quick shove might have brought me pain instead of the pleasure I received when he entered me. I had two hard cocks in me at the same time, and the feeling was incredible. I had the strongest climax of my life. It was totally fantastic and I wanted it to go on and on, but I knew I couldn't. Even in the almost mindless bliss I was experiencing, I still had a small portion of my brain trained on the clock. I had to finish this and get home.

"Fuck me, fuck me hard, fuck me hard and make me cum" I chanted as I urged the two men on and I came one more time as the two men exploded inside me. I felt John's cock pulse as he pushed his load deep into my ass, and seconds later, Bill flooded my pussy. I held still to luxuriate in the feeling, and then I said:

"That's enough sweeties. I'd love to stay longer, but I need to get on home and fix my husband's dinner."

"You going to feed him our cream pies?"

"Good heavens no."

"Why not?"

"Because my being that wet might make him suspicious and we don't want that, do we? We certainly don't want anything to put a stop to what we are doing, right."

"No, I guess not."

The two men dressed and left and I rushed to the bathroom to shower and douche before getting dressed and going home.

That's it boys and girls, one more true adventure in the life of Cyber Slut Wife. Stay tuned for the next time this bored housewife spreads her legs for some fun.

*****

I clicked on the 'back' button until I got to the story index, checked to see if there were any other stories I wanted to read, found none and then signed of the Net. I checked my watch and saw that I had cut it pretty close again. Vickie was due home in fifteen or twenty minutes from one of her many church activities and I always liked to give myself a half hours leeway.

I need to get a watch with a built in alarm. The last thing I needed was for Vickie to come home and find me reading erotic stories in an Internet adult web site. I had pretty much run out of patience with my wife, another argument and preaching session could very well end our marriage.

It was a story that a hundred thousand people could identify with. They were childhood sweethearts going steady all the way through high school, separated by college, and were brought back together four years later. They got married, had three kids who are now grown and out on their own, and a wife with suddenly nothing to do to keep her occupied.

Most wives in those circumstances went out to see if they could get back into the work force or join a charitable organization and donate time. That might have been the route that Vickie would have taken if circumstances had been different.

I still don't know how it happened. I went away for a two week training session and when I got home, I found that in my absence, Vickie had been SAVED! Washed in the blood of The Lamb, had accepted Jesus as her Lord and Master and I'm here to tell you that there is no greater fanatic in the world than the recently converted.

I pulled into the garage, got my suitcases out of the trunk and noticed a box with my Penthouse, Playboy, Gallery and other men's magazines sitting next to the trashcans. Something else didn't look right in the garage and it took me a minute before I realized that all my girlie calendars were missing from the walls.

I walked into the house and found Vickie sitting at the kitchen table reading a Bible. The girlie posters and magazines slipped to the back of my mind, as I went over and kissed her. Instead of getting up so we could hug and kiss each other, she turned her head so that my kiss just brushed her cheek. Not the greeting I had expected from a loving wife after a two week separation.

"Come on sweetie," I said, "Let's go upstairs, I'll unpack and we can make up for some lost time."

"No Burt. I think you better sit down. We need to talk."

"About what?"

"About God Burt, and how we have not let Him into our lives. When was the last time you went to church Burt?"

"I don't know. When I was twelve or thirteen I'd guess."

"Why did you turn your back on God then?"

"That is probably because I came to realize that God was just a figment of imagination for some people. That he didn't exist or if he did, he wasn't worth paying attention to."

"My God Burt, how can you say that?"

"Easy Vickie, all I have to do is look around and see how screwed up the world is. If God so loved us that He gave us his only begotten Son, he would not have let this world get into the horrible shape it is in."

"That is not God's fault Burt, that is the fau…."

"Park it Vickie. I don't argue religion with anyone. If they believe in God, nothing I say is going to change their mind and there isn't anything they can say to me that is going to change mine. What the hell is this all about Vick?"

It turns out that while I was gone, some bible thumpers came through the neighborhood knocking on doors and Vickie, tired of sitting home alone watching television, invited them in.

"I've asked God to forgive me for walking away from Him all those years ago. I've joined a church Burt and I've decided that I'm going to devote my free time working for the church and helping to spread the Gospel."

She picked up a piece of paper from the table and handed it to me.

"Here is our schedule honey. We have a Bible study on Tuesday and Thursday. There are other church activities scheduled for other nights of the week, but we will ease into them later. There are two services on Sunday, one at nine and one at eleven. I prefer the early service, but in truth, it wouldn't hurt us to go to both. Of course you will need to give up your Sunday golfing.

"There have to be some other changes made around here and I've already started. I've gotten rid of your filthy magazines and I've pulled that trash off the walls of the garage. Oh, and all of those filthy videos have been tossed out. We also need to decide how much we are going to contribute to the church. The accepted standard is ten percent, but with the children gone, I think we can do better than that."

She looked at me expectantly and I took a deep breath and wondered where to start, when suddenly it occurred to me that anything I said was going to lead to an argument that could not have any winner. I did the only thing I could think of that would make my position clear without words. I got up, went out into the garage, picked up the box of magazines and carried them back into the house. I took them into the den where I had set up a home office and I set the box down on my desk. Then I went back into the kitchen, got my suitcase, and headed for the bedroom. I was unpacking my bags when Vickie came into the bedroom.

"Why did you do that?"

"Why did I do what?"

"Bring those filthy books back into this house."

"You forgot something Vickie. Those are my magazines, not yours, and you can't throw away my stuff without talking to me first."

"I won't have that garbage in my house Burt."

"It is my house too Vick and I will have what I want in it. We might as well get this over with now. I wasn't going to say anything and just hope that it would go away, but that is unrealistic of me because it isn't going to go away. First off, I am an agnostic. I question the existence of God, but even if there is a supreme being, I have no use for him, her, or it.

"Secondly, I am not working my butt off to make money to give to a bunch of religious zealots. If you want to contribute, it will be out of your household allowance. You can give up your beauty shop appointments for God.

"Lastly, I will not be attending the Bible study, nor will I be attending any church services. All I am willing to do is go with you to church social events like potluck suppers or picnics. If you want to be a religious nut, go ahead but leave me out of it."

She looked at me for a moment and then she went over to the bed and took the pillow from the side she slept on, and started out of the room. She stopped at the door, turned to me, and said:

"I'll be sleeping in Krisha's old room, until you come to your senses" and then she left.

That move ended our marriage. It went on, but after her changing bedrooms, all we were are just two people co-existing in the same house.

*****

For the next six months, all we were are civil to each other. Vickie slept in Krisha's room and I slept in what used to be ours. It wasn't easy on me, but it wasn't a major hardship either. Like a lot of couples who had been together over twenty-five years, we grew less passionate, but more comfortable with each other. The sex had been good, but infrequent, and done only maybe five or six times a month. I did miss it, but I wasn't going to die because it stopped.

What I did miss was the snuggling, the cuddling, and the waking up in each other's arms. I hated that Vickie was depriving me of it, but at the same time, I was questioning whether she had ever really loved me if she could do this to me, to us. We grew farther and farther apart.

Vickie continued her assault on my wicked ways. The box of magazines disappeared again, but I said nothing. All they were was symbolic and the only reason I had carried them back into the house was to make a point that obviously hadn't been taken. I'd already read them and was about to throw them out.

It was about six weeks, before I noticed that I hadn't received my subscriptions of Playboy and Penthouse Letters. I found out that Vickie was throwing them away when she picked up the mail every day. I let it slide because it didn't really matter all that much to me any more – I had found the Net! More specifically, I had found thousands of porn sites that offered me everything that I had gotten from my magazines and much, much more.

It didn't take me long to realize that just as my magazines had disappeared, so would my computer if Vickie found out what I was using it for. I would just buy another one and another after that if I had to, but it could get expensive after a while. The only other option was to end the farce that our marriage had become, but to me that was the least attractive way to go. It would mean giving up my settled existence. The house would have to be sold and the proceeds need to be split. Everything else, savings, certificates of deposit, my pension, and 401k would be split fifty-fifty. I would probably end up paying alimony. It would mean giving up my wood working shop in the basement, and the three car garage which would leave me without a place to work on the '34 Ford three window coupe I was restoring. Loss of the house would inconvenience me in a lot of other ways also, so to me the solution was to just stay out of Vickie's way and not give her anything to bitch about.

As far as the Net was concerned, my thing was erotic stories and I quickly found several sites that were free, some were so-so, some were good, and a few were excellent. I was soon spending all my time on three sites. Before long, I had a list of favorite authors and one of them was Cyber Slut Wife. Her stories were a series (if she could be believed) of the sexual encounters she'd had.

Her first story described her fucking her husband's best man, just before the wedding ceremony. Next were three men she slipped away with, while on her honeymoon. It was then followed by years of hanging horns on her husband with almost every friend he had, and a whole host of others. She seduced her paperboy, the home handy man who did some work in her basement, the cable guy, door to door salesmen and even a Jehovah's Witness. Each occasion fired her up for the next and she merrily went about screwing everything in pants, until the day she thought she'd been caught. She worked her way through it unscathed and then backed off, to let things settle down. Outside of an occasional back seat visit at a party or a bar pick up when hubby was out of town, she kept her legs closed until her kids were grown and had moved out.

With the house empty now, she had time to get back to what she liked to do most – fuck! She dressed herself up and went out of the hotel at the airport, and let herself get picked up by a traveling businessman. She spent four hours in a hotel room with him and then went home and cooked her husband's dinner. Her next story told how she had done the same thing once a week for the next three weeks. On the third week, she was in the man's room in mid-fuck, when another man came into the room and decided to join them. It was her first threesome and she loved it.

The second man told her he would be back on town the following week, and he asked if he could see her again. Her next story covered that visit. She met him at nine in the morning and by noon, she just knew how big a slut she was. He brought in a friend and then a second one, and she had her first triple penetration.

One of the men brought in, was a local man named Harry and as the four of them were dressing, the local guy had suggested that they could help each other. He had customers and clients that she could take care of which would eliminate her having to troll for fresh meat and she would be able to stop going to places where someone who knew her might see her. He would get her a cell phone that only he would have the number. He would give her clothing allowance, so she could keep herself in sexy things and 'come fuck me' high heels and the biggie – he would rent her an apartment where she could 'entertain'. She thought it over and said yes.

Her latest story was about a six-man gangbang that took place when Harry hosted a poker game at the apartment. When it was over, one of the men had asked her if her husband was going to notice how loose and sloppy she was, and she replied:

"He hasn't had me in almost a year, so he'll never know."

"He hasn't fucked you in over a year? What is wrong with him?"

"Just stupid I guess."

I don't know why I was so into the Cyber Slut Wife stories. She was not the kind of women that I would like, if I met her in person. The casual way she cheated on her husband and the callous way she always referred to him, painted the portrait of a woman who was trash to my way of thinking. I think the reason I liked her stories was because they were just that, stories. She built a story around each meeting she had and included all kinds of details. None of that "I sucked his cock and then I fucked him and went home" kind of stuff.

*****

It had been fourteen months, since Vickie had moved out of our bedroom and neither one of us had made a move toward reconciliation. Things might have gone on that way for another fourteen months if only Vickie didn't have an accident. I was at work when the call from my daughter came. She had stopped by the house to visit Vickie, and had found her unconscious at the foot of the steps. Vickie had apparently fallen down the stairs and smacked her head a good one.

Krisha had called 911 and Vickie was on her way to the emergency room at County General. By the time I got there, she had been looked at and admitted. I talked with the doctor who told me that she had a concussion. X-rays had shown there was no bone damage:

"But we want to keep her overnight and take a fresh look in the morning."

"Thank you doctor. I'll go see her now."

"She's asleep right now. She was causing some problems and we had to sedate her."

"What kind of problems?"

"She was fighting the nurses and orderlies, trying to get away from them. She kept yelling that she had to get home before her husband."

"Odd. That doesn't sound like Vickie. Normally, she couldn't care less if she was home when I got there or not. That bump on her head must have made her delirious."

"That's kind of what we thought too and that's why we sedated her and want to keep her here for observation."

I did check on Vickie, but she was definitely out of it, so I went on home.

*****

The first thing I noticed is the blood spots on the carpets at the foot of the stairs, and I made a mental note to get a carpet cleaner to clean it up. The second thing didn't register right away. I didn't notice it, until I was ready to sit down and eat what I had fixed myself for dinner. There was a laptop sitting on the dining room table. I didn't even know that Vickie had one. It was open and plugged in and curiosity got the best of me.

The screen saver was running and I hit ENTER and the last thing Vickie was working on, appeared on the screen. I suddenly knew what was behind Vickie's panic attack at the hospital, and the reason why she needed to beat me home. There on the screen, was a picture of a naked Vickie with a black cock sticking in her cunt. The picture didn't show her face, but I didn't need a face to know it was her. Plainly visible were the two tattoos that she had gotten on her thirty-fifth birthday; a heart with my initials in it just above the hair line of her cunt, and a butterfly on the upper curvature of her right breast.

I sat down and started looking through the contents. Luckily, nothing was password protected and what I found turned my world on end. The first thing I found out was that the picture was an attachment from an email that Vickie had sent or was about to send before her accident stopped her. The email itself said:

"That's for your support sweetie. Here is a little something to remind you to keep sending me good comments. Love ya, CSW."

I wondered what CSW meant. I was familiar with LOL and some others, but I had never seen CSW before. Next, I checked "Sent Messages" and found forty-six more emails that all said "thanks for your support" and all had attachments.

"My Pictures" was next and it was a revelation. There were over a hundred pictures of a naked Vickie and in all of them. She had a cock either in her mouth, her ass, or her cunt. In several, she had more than one in her. The ones that showed a cock in her mouth had her face blurred, but I could still tell it was her by the tattoos. A close examination of the pictures showed that there were at least fourteen different men enjoying themselves at my expense.

A trip to "My Videos" allowed me to see Vickie being an absolute slut. In thirty-one video clips, she was fucked in all three holes, and in a couple of clips, she was taken in all three at once.

The mother lode was in "My Documents" and it was there that I learned the meaning of CSW. There, on the hard drive, was every story that Cyber Slut Wife had written, including a few that I had not yet read. My own wife was one of my favorite authors and the stories she wrote were of the things she had been doing behind my back. I'd even gotten myself off to a couple of them and wasn't that a kick in the teeth.

But even that, wasn't the best part. The best part was a folder labeled "My Diary." It was an itemized account of every sexual affair that Vickie had engaged in. It gave the listed names, dates, time, places and critique inclusion of the session. It started two days before our wedding and ran until the day before the accident. Her first encounter was my cousin Tom on the night of our rehearsal dinner. Her second was my best man, the morning of the wedding. According to her diary, there were seven other men who enjoyed her on our honeymoon when she wasn't being enjoyed by me. According to the story she wrote about it, there were only three and I wondered about that. I guess she must have thought seven would be a little unbelievable for a new bride on her honeymoon.

I found out that she considered my best friend a 'lousy fuck' and my brother 'adequate." I was totally surprised to see that she considered me 'exceptional." If that was the case, why was I only one of the hundreds who had used her, and why hadn't we been having more sex the last couple of years?

I found out that my daughter Krisha had been fathered by my about to become ex-best friend, and that I might, only might, be the father of Darlene and William.

It was much too fast. There was still a ton of stuff to read, but I couldn't take the time to do it. I needed to get back to the hospital and be there when Vickie woke up. Fortunately, Vickie's laptop had a CD burner and I got some blank CDs and downloaded everything. Leaving the laptop where it was, I headed back to County General.

*****

I was sitting in the room reading a book, when Vickie woke up. She was a little groggy at first and when she finally got around noticing me, her face registered alarm.

"How long have you been here?"

"Since it happened, Krisha found you, she called me and I came straight from work."

"You haven't been home yet?"

"No, not yet."

I saw the relief wash over her face. Just then, Krisha came in and I got up and went to the bathroom. When I came back, Krisha was gone and I asked where she was, Vickie told me that she had just stopped by to check on things and her boyfriend had been downstairs waiting so she left. I stayed for another fifteen minutes, then I said I needed to get home to feed the cat, but Vickie stopped me and gave me a list of people to call to let them know what happened. I said I would and started to leave, again and again she stopped me and asked me to talk to the doctor before I left. It was obvious that she was trying to keep me from going home. It was another hour before I was able to get out of the hospital, and when I got home, I was not surprised to see that the laptop was gone.

The doctor told me that they would be releasing Vickie around two that afternoon, so that gave me three hours to be nosey. I searched her car and found an overnight bag with two pair of high heels, some nylons, a garter belt, and a lot of make-up. I really didn't expect to find much because if her stories were true, and I didn't doubt them for one minute, most of the incriminating stuff would be at the apartment Harry had rented for her. In the closet in her bedroom, I found the carrying case for the laptop, two boxes of blank CDs and some manuals. I didn't disturb them; there was no way I wanted Vickie to know that I was on to her.

I headed for my computer to spend some time on the stuff I had downloaded. The one thing that had bothered me most since finding her laptop and seeing what was on it, was trying to reconcile Vickie's religious conversion with her whorishness. I found the answer in the information I had downloaded. In her diary, she described how Harry had told her not to have sex with me anymore. He told her that she belonged to him now and not me.

Vickie's religious conversion was a fake! It was a wedge she could use to split us apart and keep us apart. It was the old use of sex as a weapon. Withhold it until you get what you want and then give it as a reward. In my case, Vickie knew I'd never give in on the subject of religion. All her bible study classes and other church activities were just her way of getting out of the house so she could spread her legs for whoever Harry pointed her to.

*****

That afternoon, I picked Vickie up at the hospital and brought her home. I didn't do anything out of the ordinary. And as far as Vickie could tell, I wasn't the least bit suspicious of anything. I spent two days going over everything I had downloaded from her laptop and thinking about what to do. I finally made an appointment with a lawyer and he gave me the bad news. In our state, any divorce was going to cause a 50/50 split of the assets regardless of the reason for the divorce and I, in all likelihood, would have to pay for both lawyers, Vickie's and mine. The only way I could get out and keep what I wanted was to find a way to make Vickie walk away without a fight. What I had to do was sue for divorce, ask for what I wanted and not have her contest it.

I spent another week thinking on it, and I came up with a plan. It left a sour taste in my mouth to have to do it the way I was going to have to, but it was the only way for me to come out ahead on the deal. I hired a private investigator and told him what I wanted. Three weeks later, I had most of what I needed. I had all the information on Harry, I had the address of the apartment, and I had the personal information on twenty-seven of Harry's clients who had visited the apartment. One of the most interesting of those names was Thomas Shift, our city manager.

The next step was to find a twenty-four hour locksmith. One night after Vickie had fallen asleep, I took her keys from her purse and went to the locksmith and had them duplicated. I already knew from the detective's report that the apartment wasn't used when Vickie wasn't there, so I took the duplicate keys and paid the apartment a visit.

The apartment closets held enough sexy lingerie to fill a Victoria's Secret store and enough pairs of high heels to outfit a Vegas chorus line. One of the bedrooms was locked, and I found the key that opened it and I let myself in. There was a see through mirror mounted on one wall that allowed you to watch what was going on in the next bedroom. There were also three video cameras set up to tape the action. In the bedroom closet, I found over a hundred videotapes. I'd seen enough to give me an idea on how to go about getting Vickie to fade away quietly.

*****

That Friday evening when I got home from work I walked into the house to shouts of, "Surprise, surprise." Vickie had thrown a surprise birthday party for me and it was most interesting to me to see the assembled guests. Besides our three kids, there were fourteen couples, three guys without dates, seventeen men and every fucking one of them was an entry in Vickie's diary. There was a lot of glad handing, back slapping good cheer and at any other time with me not knowing. What I knew, it would have been a hell of a fine party.

Brian, my soon to be ex-best friend, gave me a three day all expenses paid trip to a golf course up in Breckenridge, probably to get me out of town, so he could fuck Vickie. There were other assorted gifts, but the one that caught my attention was the one from Vickie. It was a new laptop computer. There were two reasons why it grabbed my attention: I'd never shown any interest in having a laptop and I had no use for it and secondly, we were barely talking to each other so why was she spending that kind of money on me? Come to think of it, why did she even throw a party for me? It made no sense at all, but then what had recently? As I sat there and surveyed all the people laughing and having a good time, I wondered how many would still be laughing after I lowered the boom.

*****

It took three weeks to get all the paperwork done, and then I was ready. It was all a matter of timing. On Tuesday night, I used my duplicate set of keys to enter Vickie's love pad and I removed all the videotapes, the video cameras, and anything else I thought I might like. That night at home, I snuck into Vickie's bedroom and got her laptop from where she stored it in the closet, and put it in the trunk of my car with everything I'd taken from her apartment.

Eight o'clock the next morning, I was in Harry's office and I asked his secretary to tell him that Vickie Boland's husband was there to see him on a matter of great importance. She did and he stalled me long enough to try and call Vickie and find out what was going on. He didn't reach her because when I left the house, I cut the phone line and I had taken her cell from her purse. Finally, I felt that I had waited long enough and I told his secretary to tell him he had two minutes and then I would be leaving and my next visit would be to Thomas Shift.

That got him off the dime, and I was ushered into his office. "What is this all about Mr. Boland?"

"Saving your miserable fucking ass Mr. Grant."

"Just what are you getting at" he snarled at me and started to get up.

"You get out of that chair fuck face and I'll the beat the fuck out of you and throw you out your office window and laugh as you make the four story trip down to the street."

He sat back down and I went on, "What this is shit head is that in order to get what I want, you are going to get a free ride." I looked at my watch and said, "I'm expecting a call within the next five minutes telling me that my whorish wife has been served divorce papers. You will then see to it that she does not contest the divorce. In return, none of the videotapes that used to be in your little love nest will become public and embarrass your clients. I'm sure that Tom Shift, for one, will appreciate you seeing to it that the tapes never see the light of day. But then he doesn't know about them does he? At least he doesn't know about them yet.

"In addition to the tapes not becoming public" and I handed him a folder, "Vickie's diary will not see the light of day. If you are unable to convince her to walk away from me without a fight, it will all go public. Your business goes into the shitter to say nothing of all the personal lawsuits that will be filed against you, including one by me for alienation of affection and whatever else my lawyer can come up with."

Just then my cell phone beeped, and I took the call. When I disconnected, I said:

"The papers have been served. You probably won't hear from her until she can get to a phone – I disconnected the one at the house and I have her cell in my briefcase – but as soon as she does reach you it would be in your best interests to start on getting her not to contest the divorce."

"Just how in the hell am I supposed to be able to talk her into not contesting?"

"Your problem, not mine. You told her to stop having sex with me anymore and she did what you told her. You better hope she listens to you this time too. If worst comes to worst, I don't care if you have to kill her to save yourself, just let me know ahead of time, so I can have an iron clad alibi."

I got up to leave and when I got to the door, I stopped, turned, and said:

"I owe you a lot of pain and I am torn between hurting you bad or letting you walk in order to get what I want. You need to keep that in mind when you are trying to get her to not contest the divorce. Fail and my fallback position is to ruin you professionally, personally, financially, and physically. Imagine yourself in a wheelchair for the rest of your life and it just might help give you an incentive."

*****

I was no sooner in the car, when my cell went off again. The screen showed it was from an unregistered number. I figured that Vickie had gotten another phone, so I didn't take the call. She called several times over the next two hours, and I finally shut off the phone.

At one, I showed up at the house with a rented U-Haul van. Vickie was on me, as soon as I was in the door. She was waving the papers at me, demanding to know what I thought I was doing.

"I decided that it was time to end this farce of a marriage. When you moved out of our bedroom, you showed me you didn't want me. I finally decided that I don't want you, so I'm getting a divorce."

"Bullshit. All you ever had to do to get me out of Krisha's room and back into ours, was meet me half way on getting back in touch with God."

"You knew that would never happen Vickie, in fact you were counting on it."

"What are you talking about?"

"Doesn't matter Vick. You want to help me move your clothes and stuff out to the van, or are you comfortable with the idea I can do it without trashing most of it."

"Move my stuff to the van? Why?"

"I'm throwing you and your Bible out Vick."

"You can't do that. I've as much right to stay in this house as you have."

"That may be Vick, but you will have to get a lawyer and have him get in touch with my lawyer to establish that. Until that happens, you are out. Now, you want your stuff with you when you leave or do you want me to just push you out the door?"

"You can't do this to me."

"Oh yes I can. Now start grabbing your stuff or I'm throwing you out without it."

"Where am I supposed to go?"

"I'll drive you over to your fuck pad on Newark Circle. When you get there, you can call Harry and cry on his shoulder."

At the mention of the apartment on Newark Circle and of Harry's name, the fight went out of her. She went upstairs and started carrying things down and out to the van. I helped her and we were about halfway done, when I saw her looking anxious. She kept digging in the closet and I finally said:

"It isn't there. My lawyer has it. You will get it back when the divorce is final. He is going to use what is on it for evidence. When you get to your love nest on Newark, you can call Harry and he'll tell you all about it."

No more words were said as we finished loading her stuff into the van and nothing was said as I drove her to the apartment. I emptied the van onto the sidewalk in front of the apartment building and drove away leaving her standing there.

*****

The hardest part for me was telling the kids. Vickie was lying trash, so I couldn't just let her tell them her version which would no doubt paint me as "Attila The Hun". I had no intention playing the "pit mommy against daddy" game, but I was going to give them all the information that I had, and then let them make up their own minds.

I called Krisha at work and asked her to meet me for a drink when she got off. I told her that I was divorcing her mother, but I didn't tell her why. I gave her a copy of everything I had taken from Vickie's computer; pictures, video clips, diary – all of it – and told her to go through it and that if she had any questions to give me a call or come by the house and see me.

"I'll be home all weekend 'pumpkin' (my pet name for her) if you want to talk."

Next, I called Darlene and William and made arrangements to meet them for breakfast at Denny's. I gave them the same talk that I gave Krisha, gave them copies of the same stuff, and went on home.

Darlene was the first to call. She called around noon, "Surely you don't believe any of that stuff, do you dad?"

"I'm afraid I believe all of it honey."

"It can't be true dad. There must be a reasonable explanation for it. Maybe it was an outline for a book or something. She always said she was going to write someday."

"Have you gone through all the material yet?"

"No, not yet."

"You remember the night your mother took you and Krisha into our bedroom and showed you her new tattoos?"

"Yes, I remember that Krisha and I thought it was a real kick."

"Finish all the material honey. Check out My Pictures and My Videos. You will recognize the tattoos."

"You are wrong about this dad, I just know you have to wrong. Mom couldn't do this, she just couldn't."

"I'm sorry honey, but I have to go now. I'll be home all day if you want to talk when you finish the material."

*****

I was sitting on the couch in the living room reading, when Krisha came into the house. She came into the room and sat down on a chair opposite me. I put the book down and waited. She looked down at the floor for a moment and then asked:

"Is it true?"

"Is what true honey?"

"That Brian is my father?"

"I only know what your mother wrote in her diary."

"How long have you known?"

"Since the day she fell down the steps" and I went on to explain how I'd come into the house and found the laptop and what I'd done after.

"That computer? I guess it was a good thing I didn't take the time to look at what was on it. God only knows what I would have done."

"I don't understand?"

"That day in the hospital. When you left the room, mom asked me to do her a favor. She said she had gotten you a laptop for your birthday and had set it up to check it out before giving it to you. She wanted me to run back to the house and get it, before you got home and saw it. She said she would keep you busy to give me time. I didn't take the time to look at it, because I thought you might be right behind me. I put it in the trunk of my car until mom called and asked me to bring it to her."

"I guess that explains the one I got for my birthday. After her story to you, she had to give me one or you might have wondered and maybe asked about it or maybe you might have thought she had given it to me early and asked me how I liked it."

"I can't believe she was that way, and for all those years. You never suspected?"

"No, I didn't have a clue."

There were several moments of silence between us, and then Krisha said:

"Brian is not my dad you know, you are. You always have been and you always will be."

Another period of silence and then the tears started flowing, and she cried out "Daddy" and got up and came over and threw herself in my arms. She sobbed into my shoulder for a long time and between sobs, she kept repeating over and over:

"How could she do that to you, to us."

*****

William was the pragmatic one. He called around five that afternoon.

"I've got a nine o'clock tee time in the morning. Fell like having your butt whipped?"

"Yeah, I can make it, but your game better be good because my putting has been killer lately."

"I'll pick you up at eight."

The first couple of minutes of the drive, were filled with an awkward silence and then William said:

"How do we handle this?"

"How do we handle what?"

"She's my mother and I love her. You are my father and I love you. I'm not happy with what she has done to the family, but I am not going to turn my back on her. I will try and be there for her if she needs me. The same goes for you. Is my relationship with her going to be a problem, as far as you are concerned?"

"Of course not. Just because I have no use for her, doesn't mean everyone else has to feel the same way."

"Good."

We played eighteen and he did indeed whip my ass. The diary

entry that he might or might not be my son, was never mentioned by either of us.

*****

Darlene was the disappointment. She held it against me that I had exposed her mother's flaws to her and I ended up being the bad guy as far as she was concerned. I don't know if that rift will ever heal.

*****

Two weeks went by with no word from Harry or Vickie, as to whether or not she was going to contest the divorce so I started preparing for the worst. In keeping with my promise to ruin Harry if he didn't convince Vickie to walk away, I started to watch the videotapes to see just what I had to work with. I was amazed at what I found. Besides the city manager, I found two councilmen and one county commissioner – all married – and several prominent local businessmen, also all married.

There was tape on eleven of the seventeen assholes that were at my party and another eleven that I knew fairly well. The rest of the men on the tapes I didn't recognize, but it didn't matter, I had more than enough for what I was going to do.

It suddenly occurred to me that I would have no leverage if Harry somehow got the tapes back. I did have a copy of Vickie's diary but it could always be claimed that I made it up myself. I needed the visual proof so I got all of the tapes together and got them out of the house and hid them. Before I did that, I copied the portions of the tapes that showed the twenty-two supposed friends of mine and I began making up packages to give to their wives and girlfriends. The package included the video of the asshole and Vickie's diary entries that pertained to him.

Once the packages were ready, I called Harry, and his secretary wouldn't put me through to him, so I asked her to give him a message.

"Tell him that since I haven't heard from him, I'm going to start putting out some of the information I have. I'm going to do my so-called friends first and that if I have not heard from him by Friday, I will be calling on the wives of Thomas Minor, Gregg Silverman, and Craig Staub. Those visits will be followed by visits to the wives of four politicians. He will know the ones I'm talking about."

By Thursday, I had hand delivered the twenty-two packages to the wives and girlfriends of the twenty-two assholes. Also by Thursday, I had received seven phone calls from ex-friends who swore they were going to get me for ruining their marriages. My response to all of them was the same:

"Hey fuckhead, you fucked my wife, I didn't fuck yours. You ruined your own fucking marriage, not me, and if you come for me, bring lots of help because I have a lot of anger I need to take out on someone and you'll fill the bill just fine."

Nevertheless, I started carrying a handgun under the front seat of my car.

Friday morning, I was busy building the packages for the wives and girlfriends of the eight ex-friends, I didn't have video on. I'd printed out the diary entries that pertained to them and I made eight tapes that showed Vickie with mutual friends. The idea was that I could say:

"Here is her dairy information on him. I don't have actual tape of him with Vickie, but here is a tape showing you what she was doing with the others. If you want to give him a pass that is your business, but at least I gave you warning that you should get yourself tested for STDs as soon as possible."

I had just finished the packages, when the phone rang. It was Harry.

"She had agreed. What now?"

"Have her go see my lawyer. I'll give her until Tuesday. After that I won't hold back."

"You know what you've done to her? She's afraid to go out anymore. There are a dozen people looking for her with mayhem on their minds."

"Not my problem. It wouldn't bother me any if some of them got a hold of her."

"You really hate her that much?"

"No, actually I don't hate her that much. I hate her hell of a lot more."

"What happens after she sees the lawyer?"

"I'll give her back her computer, but I will sit on everything else until the divorce is final. If the divorce goes off without a hitch, I'll return everything I took out of the apartment."

"After making copies?"

"For my protection against reprisals, I will copy the tapes of the four politicians and two of the most prominent businessmen."

"That isn't very trusting of you."

"I trusted my wife and look what that got me."

*****

I spent the rest of Friday handing out the last eight packages and on Saturday, I had the kids over for a barbecue. In the middle of it, Darlene pulled me aside and tried to talk me into letting her mother move back in the house and when I said no way, she left in a huff. The other two watched her go and just shrugged their shoulders.

My standing golf date for Sunday was cancelled, since two of the foursome were ex-friend whose wives received a package from me. Sometimes it just sucks to be me.

Monday at two in the afternoon, my lawyer called me and told me that Vickie had just been in and had signed the papers. Now, I'll just sit and wait for the divorce to become final.

I know it sounds silly to say this, but I do believe I was better off not knowing what I know now.

And I'm probably never going to read a Cyber Slut Wife story ever again.

The End

The Charitable Deed

BARRY

I think that my marriage is over. I can't be absolutely certain, until I talk with my wife, but I think that when I saw her get in that Cadillac and drive away, she was telling me goodbye. There is a saying that you hear from time to time, "No good deed goes unpunished" and it would certainly seem to be the case where I'm concerned.

Janice and I have been married just over eight years. In most of those eight years, Janice was a stay at home mom. When the two kids started school, it left her with a lot of free time on her hands. I make excellent money, so Janice didn't need to go to work, but she did want something to do, so she volunteered to work for several charities. I got used to her being gone one or two nights a week, as she became more and more involved with her volunteer work. A year went by and Janice was appointed to various committees and the committees claimed more and more of her time. I found myself being dragged from one charitable function after another, and it got to the point where I finally had to buy a tux rather than keep on renting them. There were endless fifty and one hundred-dollar plate dinners to benefit this worthy cause and that worthwhile charity, and I came to hate the taste of chicken. Then came the day that Janice was made the chairwoman of a committee (which shall remain nameless to protect the identities of the guilty parties), and things got even more hectic.

Another year went by and along the way Janice picked up a Woman of the Year award and several other awards for her civic accomplishments and our picture became an almost weekly occurrence on the society pages of the local newspapers. All of that exposure made other charities and fund raising groups seek out Janice to get her help. Soon, Janice was spending almost every night of the week working for one group or another. Saturday night usually meant that the two of us would be at some affair or other to support some worthy cause. I was getting pretty tired of it, and I finally told her that she needed to cut back on what she was doing so that the two of us could spend some time together alone. I pointed out that our sex life had become almost nonexistent and that I was unhappy about it. Janice promised me that she would eliminate some of her activities, but before she could do it she was tapped to be the chairwoman of the committee that put on the local charities biggest money raising event of the year. The event had been put on every year for the past fifteen years, and had never failed to raise tons of money. It was a date auction. Every year, one of the city's largest and most popular restaurants donated ten dinners, complete with all drinks for the auction. Then ten lovely young women volunteers were auctioned off with the dinners. The winning bidder got a dinner date with the woman he had bid on, and a local limo service donated a limo to pick the couple up and take them to dinner and then take them back home. Several of those dates had ended in marriage for the two people involved. It was the social event of the year and it was up to Janice and her committee, to see that it went off without a hitch.

It came apart on the night of the event. Janice and I had already arrived, and I was sitting and sipping a vodka martini as Janice ran around attending to last minute details. She finally managed to find time to sit down with me and have a drink. As we were sitting there, Toni came up and sat down with us.

"We have a problem Janice."

"What's wrong?"

"Four of the girls who volunteered for the auction have called and cancelled."

"Why?"

"Sue Wilson is stuck in Kansas City. The airport is weathered in and she can't get a flight out. Mary Miller is in the hospital with a burst appendix and two others are down with the flu that has been going around."

"Oh shit! It's too late to find replacements. Why the hell does this have to happen the year I'm involved with this?"

"Well, a couple of us have come up with a solution to the problem. It's drastic, but we can make it work if we can get some cooperation."

"From who?"

Tina looked over at me and said, "From you and your husband."

"What do you mean?" Janice asked.

"Liz got her fiancée to agree to let her be one of the replacements and I talked my boyfriend into letting me be on. Helen's husband is willing to let her do it, but only on one condition."

"And that condition?"

"That you take the fourth spot."

"Why me?"

"A married woman has never been auctioned off before and he doesn't want Helen to be the first, and more specifically, the only one. He says people might take it wrong if it were only Helen, but he thinks that if there are two of you, things will be okay."

I knew that Janice would be in a panic to save her event, so I wasn't surprised when both women turned to me. "Oh no" I said, "I don't think so."

"Why not?" Tina wanted to know. "It's only a dinner date. The limo picks her up, takes her to the restaurant, she has drinks, dinner, dances a little and then the limo brings her home and drops her at your door."

"I'm sorry girls, but I can't see letting my wife go out on a date with another man. Get someone else on the committee to do it."

"Like who, Angela Parker? Who in their right mind would pay a dime to take her out? Betty Pierpoint? Sixty years old, blue hair, and a face like a dried raisin? Boy wouldn't she bring in the big bucks."

The two of them spent the next ten minutes hammering at me. What the hell, it was for a good cause, right? So I did my good deed for the charity and said okay.

After the cocktail hour dinner was served and during the entire meal, not a word was said between Janice and me. In fact, Janice couldn't even bring herself to look at me. I'm pretty sure that she was having second thoughts about things, but was afraid to let me know it. I figured that she was between a rock and a hard place - she knew I didn't want her to do it, she was thinking she shouldn't do it, but she couldn't bear the thought that the night would be less than successful under her management. After dinner, the auction started and things seemed to be going smoothly. The first eight young ladies were auctioned off for some pretty hefty amounts; the lowest went at eighteen hundred and the highest for twenty-three. Then the auctioneer called for the next volunteer to come up to the auction stand. There was a gasp from the crowd as Helen stood up and went to the auction block. At least half the crowd there that night knew that Helen was married and her appearance on the stand caused quite a stir. I was somewhat surprised when Helen only brought in eleven hundred. I wondered if it was because she was married, was five years older than the previous eight young ladies or both. Then it was Janice's turn. Her appearance on the stand caused just as big a stir as Helen's did. The bidding got off to a good start, but bogged down at a thousand dollars. Then from the back of the room came a booming "Eleven hundred." When no one topped that offer, I saw Janice look beseechingly at me and I knew what she was thinking - "Save me!" - was written all over her face. The bidder in the back of the room was Jason North.

Some explanation here. Janice is Southern born and bred. Her family back home in South Carolina is a bit on the racist side and Janice went off to college with all the baggage that a family full of racists could give her. Her four years in college went a long way toward modifying her attitudes toward minorities, but Janice still was never comfortable around them in a social context. Jason was black. Not only that, but Janice and Jason had a history. Not much of one, but more than enough to make Janice nervous. Jason and I used to work for the same company and at one company Christmas party Jason had asked Janice to dance and Janice had said no. Janice had already danced with half of the men I work with, and her refusal to dance with Jason was taken by him as a racial gesture. Later that night, there was another incident that cemented in Jason's mind that Janice was a bigot. Jason caught Janice underneath the mistletoe and kissed her. Janice had been kissed under that piece of greenery by at least a dozen other men that night, but when Jason kissed her she shoved him away and ran to the ladies room. Janice said that she suddenly had to pee, but Jason just knew that it was so she could wash the touch of him off of her. Shortly after that, Jason left the company to go into business for himself and now here he was trying to buy a date with a white woman he considered a closet racist. And there was my wife, eyes pleading with me to do something to stop it.

I bid twelve hundred and then Jason and I swapped bids until Jason followed my bid of two thousand with a bid of twenty-five hundred and at that point, I decided to bail out. It was obvious to me that Jason was going to go as high as necessary to win and I couldn't see spending a fortune just to take my own wife to dinner. Besides, Janice needed to get over being nervous about being around minorities. Maybe an evening of dinner and dancing with a black man would help her see that blacks were not the savages and barbarians that her parents had made them out to be.

"Twenty-five once, twenty-five twice, going, going and gone for twenty-five hundred dollars" and the gavel fell.

The ride home was quiet and Janice didn't say a word to me until we got into the house and then she let me have it.

"How could you let that asshole win? How could you let that arrogant bastard have a date with me?"

"Whoa up there lady. You seem to forget that we are not the Rockefellers or the Vanderbilt's. We may be well off, but we are by no means rich and it was obvious that Jason was going to keep on bidding until he won. Not only that, but think of the possible scandal. The most anyone has ever bid during one of those auctions was twenty-seven hundred. What if Jason, and I'm sure he would have, had gone to three or even four thousand. For a married woman? How do you think that would have played around town? Besides, you are the one who talked me into letting you do this. Remember what you said? "It's only dinner, a few drinks and some dancing. It isn't like I'm going to have an affair or anything like that." You wanted your night to be a success and it was. All you have to do now is have dinner with Jason and think about how his bid was the highest of the night and that your fund drive was a huge success."

That wasn't the end of it, of course, and things were pretty cool around our house for the next couple of days.

JASON

I couldn't believe it. I'd almost passed up on coming to this five hundred dollar plate dinner. Randy had worked on me for the better part of two weeks trying to talk me into attending the event. And it wasn't his, "Hey, you can get a date with a beautiful white chick" that finally convinced me. No, it was the fact that it was the so-called "Social Event" of the year that brought me. Meeting some of the people who attended the event might help me in my business. That and the slim chance that I might get my picture in the society pages of the morning papers which would also help me out. I was surprised to see Barry and his wife Janice sitting at the head table. God, but she was one gorgeous woman. Too bad she was a fucking bigot. I was also surprised that dinner wasn't another rubber chicken affair. They actually served a pretty good prime rib and the drinks weren't watered down either. A couple of Rum and Cokes had me in a pretty mellow mood by the time the auction started. I watched as one sexy looking white girl after another walked up front and was auctioned off for over a grand. I shook my head and wondered what kind of fool would shell out that much money just to be able to take her out to dinner. A dinner and a few dances were all he was going to get. If one of those girls ever gave it up, the resultant scandal would put an end to the charity affair. Then came my biggest surprise of the evening, Janice got up and moved to the auction block. I sat there stunned as the bidding started. Why was she doing this? Why was Barry letting her do it? I watched in fascination as men bid for the pleasure of just having dinner with this beautiful woman. The bidding started to slow down and it looked like Janice was going to go for a measly thousand dollars. This magnificent woman's worth is only a grand? Without even thinking about it, I heard myself call out eleven hundred. Janice looked my way. When she saw who it was who had bid on her, I saw the fright come over her face. I saw her look to Barry and I could read the look she gave him, "Don't let the nigger get me Barry." That look did it. I said to myself, "All right you bigoted bitch; I don't care what it costs me you WILL be sitting across from me in that restaurant. Then Barry and I started bidding against each other, until he realized that I had no intention of quitting until I won. After it was over, I walked up to the head table and in a voice loud enough for everyone to hear I said, "I'm so glad that I won the pleasure of your company. I'm free tomorrow, will that work for you?"

I got a look that would crumble a stone statue, but everyone had heard me and so she had to answer, "No, tomorrow is not a good time for me. Why don't you give me a call and we will see what we can work out."

And give you time to find a way out? Not on your life honey.

"Well if tomorrow is out we can make it Friday. That is the last day I will have available for the next couple of months. If you can't make it on Friday, I'll make it easy on you and withdraw my bid."

I saw her eyes dart around the table and she saw that every eye was on her and every ear was waiting to hear what she would say. If she said Friday was not good for her, she was through as far as her committee was concerned. These people were not stupid, they would see right through her. She looked back at me and I saw her accept her fate. "Friday will work fine for me."

"Beautiful. I'll make the reservations and pick you up around seven."

JANICE

I knew I was in trouble when I walked from the house and the black chauffeur got out and opened the limo door for me. God - all alone in the car with two black men - it couldn't have been any worse for me. One was bad enough, but two? When I settled down on the seat as close to the door and as far from Jason as possible, I told myself that I could get through the evening if I just kept my cool. Damn Barry anyway; he could have kept me from this if he wasn't so damned cheap. It was hard on me making small talk with Jason. I knew what he thought of me, but he was wrong. He didn't know it of course, but then no one else did either, not even Barry. Everyone knew my background; that my family was racists from the old school and that I had been brought up in their belief system and they all assumed that I naturally felt as my parents did. Nothing could have been farther from the truth. I hated my parents with a burning passion and if they were for something I was automatically against it, and if they were against something, I signed up for the committee that was fighting to legalize it. Why the hatred? Because my father sexually abused me, and my mother knew about it and turned a blind eye. She even went as far as to leave the house to "go shopping" when she knew it was happening. The last time my father abused me was the day I left to go to college and I set off on that journey. I was already thinking of what I could do that would someday punish both of my parents.

The opportunity came in my junior year. I was dating one of the guys on the football team and one night we were supposed to meet at a party, and when I got there, he was drunk on his ass. When the party ended, it was up to me to get Jimmy home. One of his team members offered to help me get him into the car and then out of the car at the dorm. Afterwards we went for coffee. Bobby was big, black, and he had an infectious smile and before we left Denny's, I'd agreed to go out with him. I wasn't a virgin, but I wasn't a round-heeled slut either. No boy ever got me before the sixth date, and no boy ever got a date after the third one, unless I liked him a lot. Bobby picked me up at seven and by eight-thirty, he had already fucked me twice. From that night on, Bobby and I went at it hot and heavy, and I made sure that my parents got plenty of pictures of the two of us together. At Christmas, I sent cards to all of mom and dad's neighbors - something I did every year anyway - and in each card, I included a picture of my fiancée and me hugging. My parents and I became estranged, and didn't that just break my little heart.

At the beginning of our senior year, I asked Bobby if he had given any thought to our future after graduation.

"Future? You and me? I'm afraid we don't have a future Janice."

It seems Bobby had his future all mapped out. Law school and then politics and a white wife was a baggage he didn't plan on carrying. I was crushed and we were no longer a couple. One night, Bobby showed up at a party I was attending. He smiled at me and I turned my back on him and grabbed the first guy who came along and pulled him out onto the dance floor. He was a black guy and as we were dancing he bluntly asked, "Are you one of those white girls who fantasize about black cock?"

Over his shoulder, I saw Bobby watching us and anger at him shot through me. "I don't just fantasize baby, I lust after it. Why do you think I grabbed you? You want to get lucky tonight?"

"You serious girl?"

"You got a place where we can go?"

He took me by the hand and led me up to the second floor to a bedroom. It was a no frills fuck, a blowjob to get him hard again, and then another hard and fast fuck. We returned to the party and he told one of his buddies what had happened and his buddy hit on me. When I saw Bobby glancing our way, I grabbed the guy by the hand and led him upstairs. I put out for seven black guys that night, and told two of them who were friends of Bobby's that I'd like to see them again.

It had started out as a way to get even with Bobby and then it took on a life of its own. I found that I was attracted to black men. They seemed to have some sort of animal magnetism that drew me to them. It wasn't long before I was known around campus as that "nigger loving whore" and I have to admit it was true. The night I'd let seven of them have me pretty much, set the tone for my last six months at school. I dated only blacks and at parties, I usually ended up having sex with several. One memorable night I was gangbanged by twenty-one of them. I staggered out of that bedroom and got in the tub to soak and as I relaxed in that hot soothing water, I thought about what I was doing and how destructive it was. I knew I needed to make some major changes in my life. For the rest of the term, I avoided blacks and didn't date anyone, white or black, until I graduated. I found a job and an apartment, then started out on my new career.

Over the next year, I stayed away from men and concentrated on my job. One night while I was working late, the janitor came into the room where I was working. He was a middle aged man and not particularly good looking, but he was black and the animal magnetism that I'd always felt around blacks was there and he enjoyed me right on my desk. I worked late almost every night after that, and spent a lot of time on my desk on my back. One night, about three weeks after the first time, he showed up with a couple of buddies, all black of course, and before long, I was getting gangbanged almost every night. Again, I made an attempt to gain control of my life. I quit my job and moved clear across the country to try and start over. I met Barry, fell in love, and we got married. Barry knew nothing of my past, but he did know about my racist parents. He wanted to know why I never had any contact with them, and I told him about the sexual abuse. He just assumed from my nervousness whenever I was around blacks, that I had my parent's attitude toward minorities. He couldn't have been more wrong. I was nervous around blacks because I was scared to death of what could happen.

I looked over at Jason and he smiled at me, and I felt a tingle in my crotch. A glance up front at the chauffeur showed him looking back at us and smiling. My panties got wet. Two of them, "Sweet Jesus Janice" I thought, "Keep control, be strong."

BARRY

I expected Janice to be late, so I went to bed around ten-thirty. I admit that I did it, so I wouldn't have to face her when she got home. I figured that she would be in a pissy mood after being forced to spent four or five hours with Jason and I'd just wait until the next day to get hollered again for not rescuing her. I woke up at seven and found that I was alone in bed. Great, I thought, she's so pissed that she'd rather sleep on the couch than sleep with me. I got up, took my shower and headed for the kitchen to put the coffee on. On the way, I looked in the spare bedroom, but Janice wasn't there. She wasn't on the couch either. I put the coffee on and checked out the rest of the house - no Janice! I poured myself a cup of coffee and got out the phone book and looked up the number of the limo company. I called and found out that the limo had returned at twenty after midnight. I was just picking up the phone to call the police, when I heard a car door slam and I got up and headed for the front room and got there just as Janice came through the door. She was a mess! Her nylons had runs in them and her black cocktail dress had white stains on it. I started to ask her where she'd been and she cut me off with a "Not now Barry, we'll talk later" and she hurried past me to the bedroom. I turned and started to follow her, but then stopped and went to the front window and looked out. There was a Cadillac in the drive, and I could see two men sitting on the front seat. Because of the tinted windows I couldn't make out who they were. I was debating going outside when I heard Janice come out of the bedroom and I turned and saw that she had changed into jeans and a sweatshirt. "Janice, what…" "Later Barry, I don't have time now" and she opened the front door. I reached out to grab her arm, but she dodged it and went running down the steps and then down the drive to the Cadillac. The passenger door opened and a black man got out and Janice slid into the car and was sitting between the two men when the car backed out of the drive, turned, and headed down the street. In the back of my mind, I had the feeling that I had seen the black man before and suddenly it came to me - he was the chauffeur that had picked up Janice the night before. I wondered what the hell that was all about. In the bedroom, I found that Janice had just taken off her clothes and dropped them on the floor. I picked them up to toss them into the laundry hamper, and I noticed that the crotch of her panties was soaking wet and then I noticed that the wet was slick and slimy. I raised it to my nose and sniffed, and I knew immediately what it was. Janice and I were going to have a lot to talk about when she got home, an awful lot to talk about.

The End

-
-
-
-
-
-
-
-

The Man
From Out of Town

-
-
-
-
-
-
-

I met Nancy as the result of a "kind of" blind date. It was a blind date and it wasn't. Confusing I know, but true all the same. What happened was that one of my golfing buddies invited me over to his house one Sunday for a barbecue. I had been to Glen's place several times before for pool parties and barbecues. I knew his wife Amy, and I'd always had an enjoyable time, so I said I would come,

When I got to the house, there were already a dozen people there. Glen told me I knew where the portable bar was and to go help myself. I hadn't been there twenty minutes, when Glen came up to me and told me he had somebody that he wanted me to meet. He walked me over to an absolutely stunning brunette. He introduced me to Nancy Coleman and as I was shaking her hand, I saw Amy over by the door that led into the kitchen and she was staring intently at Glen, Nancy, and me. Then Glen said:

"Excuse me if I abandon you two. Someone just came in that I have to talk to."

He walked off and I saw him say something to Amy, saw her cast a glance at Nancy and me and then go into the house. I had the sudden thought that someone was doing some "match-making" but then I discarded the thought. There was no way anyone had to find a date for Nancy. Hair below her shoulders, sparkling hazel eyes and (I was to find out later) a body that measured 34D-23-34. Nancy had to be beating off the guys with a stick.

We talked for a bit – the usual- what do you do, where do you live kind of stuff. I found out that she worked with Amy at the advertising agency and she found out that I owned a machine shop. I found out that she lived in an apartment and had never been married and she learned that I was divorced and living in the house that I had managed to keep after the dust settled. She excused herself to go and use the facilities and I went over and started talking with Sue and Alan Rogers.

I spelled Glen for a while on the grill, and then I had to go and use the bathroom. As I came down the hallway after using the john, I heard Amy talking to Glen in the kitchen.

"Did they seem to like each other?"

"How would I know Amy? What could I get out of "Rob this is Nancy, Nancy this is Rob?"

I stopped where I was and eavesdropped.

"Couldn't you tell anything from their facial expressions?"

"Get serious Amy. Rob is a guy. He had to be drooling when he saw her, but I'm not a woman so I have no idea how Nancy saw him. I still don't think we have any business meddling."

"Rob needs to come out of his shell. He needs to get over Grace and Nancy needs someone to help her put Stan behind her and I think she and Rob would make a great couple."

"Well I got him here and I introduced them, and that is as far as I'm going to go. We have other guests, so we need to get back out there."

I went outside and got another beer out of the cooler. I was standing there sipping the beer and watching the impromptu water polo game, when Amy walked up with Nancy and asked me why I wasn't in the pool playing. I waved the beer at her and said something to the effect that water and beer didn't mix all that well. Amy remarked that I was "no fun" and she walked off leaving Nancy with me. As soon as Amy was gone Nancy said:

"Have you figured it out yet?"

"Oh yeah. Glen getting me over and introducing me to you almost as soon as I walked in the door was a clue, but then I said, "No way!" A girl like you would never need to be fixed up. A girl who looked like you would have more guys hanging around than you could count. But then, I overheard Amy talking to Glen in the house."

"What did they say?"

"That I needed to come out of my shell and get over my ex-wife and that you needed some help to put some guy behind you."

"Do you?"

"Do I what?"

"Need to get over your ex-wife?"

"Not hardly. I was over her the minute I caught her cheating on me with her boss."

"Then what's with the "get you out of your shell" business?"

"Amy thinks that since I haven't dated since I divorced Grace that I'm still having trouble getting over Grace. The real reason I haven't dated is that I just have not had the time. My business has been growing and it has been taking up most of my time. I just don't have the time to go out and meet new ladies."

"Well, she has me pegged. I haven't dated in months because of coming off on a bad relationship. I've pretty much been fed up with men in general. Most of the guys I know that hit on me figure that, since I was in a relationship I'm used to having a regular diet of sex and now that I'm out of the relationship, I must be looking for a replacement so I can get back to what I was having."

"I hate to sound like a pig, but most guys who look at you are going to want to take you to the nearest bedroom. You are quite spectacular."

"Don't you think that they should at least offer to take me out to dinner and maybe a movie before dragging me to the nearest bed?"

"That bad?"

"Sometimes worse."

"I'm more of a dinner, drinks, and dancing man, and I try to stay away from bedrooms until I at least get to know the lady pretty well."

"Oh be still my beating heart. Drinks AND dancing. Where do I sign up?"

"If you are serious, I would love the honor of your company next Friday."

"Next Friday? I have to wait that long?"

"For dinner, drinks and dancing, but tomorrow is good if you are into football."

"Football?"

"I have tickets to the game tomorrow night."

"Oh you sweetie. I love watching Elway play."

"Early dinner and then Mile High?"

"You got it."

"One last thing."

"What?"

"Slap me."

"What? Why would I do that?"

"Because Amy and Glen are watching us right now and I think it would be great to twist their panties."

"But what would I tell Amy?"

"That I asked you to go home with me and do some playing in the bedroom and when Glen asks me what happened, I'll tell him the same."

"You sure you want me to do that?"

"Yeah. Slap me and then we will spend the rest of the party looking daggers at each other. But you need to do it now while they are still watching."

"Okay, if you are sure" and then she slapped me. She slapped me hard.

"Damn woman. That hurt."

"You should know this about me sweetie; I don't do anything halfway."

She stalked off giving every impression of being severally pissed. I saw Glen give Amy an "I told you we should not have meddled" look and I went and got another beer.

*****

Monday night over cheese and onion enchiladas at El Mason, Nancy asked me if Glen had asked me why she had slapped me. I grinned and then told her what happened.

"He pulled me aside and asked me just what in the hell I'd done to piss you off. I gave him the most innocent look I could muster and then said, "I don't understand it. All I did was tell her that I had purchased a new mattress for my king size bed and then asked her if she would like to come over and check it out."

Nancy laughed and said "You didn't!"

"Oh yes I did. I bet it will be a long time before they try any more match-making with me. Did they ask you why?"

"Amy intercepted me on my way to the bathroom and asked me why in the world I slapped you and I told her that you said that if I left the party with you, you would show me how good you were at giving oral sex. Her jaw looked like it was going to hit the floor."

"Well, assuming that tonight goes well and our Friday night works out, we may see them again while in each other's company. That should be something to look forward to."

The night did go well. It didn't hurt any that she liked to watch Elway play and that he was in fine form that Monday night. She was the first woman I'd ever taken to any sporting event that stood up, yelled, whistled and in general behaved like most male rabid sports fans.

Friday night went equally well. She was a dream to dance with, and I hated for the evening to end, but it ended on a high note. When I walked her to her door, she told me that she'd had a wonderful time, would love to do it again and then she kissed me. It was just a light peck on the lips, but it still made me weak in the knees. That night led to several others and as hard as it was for me to do, I behaved myself. I did not want to do anything that would scare her away.

One night, after we had been dating for a little over a month, I walked Nancy to her door, kissed her goodnight and then she surprised me by pulling me into her apartment.

"We are both grown ups Rob and we both know what we want. Since for some reason you won't make the move, I guess it is up to me."

She pulled her sweater up over her head and dropped it to the floor. She was unhooking her bra when she said:

"Am I going to be the only one undressed in this room?"

I might have been a little on the slow side, but I wasn't stupid so I started playing catch up. When she was entirely nude, I stopped undressing for a moment and took a few seconds to appreciate the sight before me – she was magnificent!

"Put your tongue back in your mouth sweetie. The bedroom is back here" and she turned and headed for a hallway.

For the next month, we kept steady company and most nights, we ended up in her bed or mine. One night we were on my bed all wrapped around each other after a rather exhausting love making session, and I said to her:

"This friends with benefits relationship is nice, but have you given any thought to something a little more permanent?"

"What do you have in mind?"

"I promised myself after Grace that I wasn't ever going to get into another committed relationship again, but then you came along. In the back of my head a little voice is screaming "Don't let her get away." I'm listening to that voice and I am agreeing with it. I would be a fool to let you get away."

"I don't know sweetie. We do seem to fit and we do seem to enjoy the hell out of each other, but making it permanent? I don't know about that."

"How about a trial period? Move in with me and let's see how living together works out."

She moved in the next day.

*****

Nancy had been living with me for just over three weeks when I invited a bunch of friends over for a Sunday barbecue. I hung a sign on the front door telling everyone to come on in and that we were out in the backyard. I was standing with my arm around Nancy and talking with Brian and Christine Moser, when Glen and Amy arrived. I just happened to be looking toward the door when they came out of the house, and I saw them see Nancy and me, and they stopped dead in their tracks and looked at each other. I nudged Nancy and nodded toward Glen and Amy, then she smiled and said:

"Show time!"

We excused ourselves from Brian and Christine, and walked over to Glen and Amy. Amy looked from Nancy to me and then back to Nancy, the confusion evident on her face.

"What can I say?" Nancy said. "The more I thought about it, the more I felt the need to know if he was as good at oral as he said he was" and she took Nancy by the arm and led her away.

Glen and I watched them walk away and then Glen gave a little laugh and said, "You old dog you" and I smiled and said, "Come on bud, let's go get us a beer."

Nancy and I lived together for six months and then one night, I asked her if she was ready to make things legal and permanent and she said she was, but she didn't want a church wedding, just a justice of the peace and then a big party in our backyard.

"Done! I'd like Glen and Amy to be there as witnesses. After all, they did make it happen."

"If she ever gotten over the shock of seeing us together."

"Yes, there is that."

We set a date two months away and then called Glen and Amy to give them the news. Two days later, Glen called me and asked me to meet him for a beer. I said okay and we set a time and a place. When I showed up, I was surprised to find Amy sitting at the table with Glen. I sat down and ordered a beer and while waiting for the waitress to bring it, Glen said:

"I'm not usually one for meddling Rob, but a friend has to watch a friend's back so Amy and I felt we had to talk with you before you and Nancy get married."

Then Amy said, "Has Nancy told you about Scott?"

"Scott? No, she has never mentioned a Scott."

"This is hard for me Rob because I really like Nancy, but Glen and I really like you too and we have known you a lot longer. I can't let you go into your marriage without making sure that your eyes are wide open. This is really, really hard for me Rob, so please don't interrupt until I get it all out and then I'll answer any questions I can. Okay?"

I nodded a yes.

"Nancy used to work at our Atlanta office. She met Scott there and the two of them fell into a hot a very steamy affair. I say affair instead of romance because Scott was married and had three kids. Anyway, the affair was so intense that it interfered with their work, and management in Atlanta told them that one of them needed to leave. Since Scott was married and owned a home, Nancy was the one to go. She transferred to my office."

"I don't see the problem Amy. What Nancy did in the past before we met is no business of mine any more than what I did before meeting her is hers."

"The problem Rob is that Scott isn't in Nancy's past. She still talks to him two or three times a week on the phone and Scott has flown into town a dozen times for meetings since Nancy moved here. I don't know that she has gotten together with him while he was here, but she is definitely more cheerful and upbeat after one of his visits."

"Again Amy; what she did before she met me is none of my business."

"Scott has been to town four times since you and Nancy got together, and the last two times were after she started living with you. The last time was just last week."

"So maybe they parted friends and they meet for lunch or coffee when he is here. I don't see that it is something that I should be concerned with."

"Fine. We just thought you should know."

"Look guys, I appreciate what you are doing here and given what went on with Grace I do have to admit to a little trepidation when it comes to getting married again, but I feel real good about Nancy and me. On the other hand, if you do think there is a possibility of there being fire where there is smoke and you come up with something definite please let me know. I've still got two months before Nancy and I do the ring thing."

*****

Three weeks went by and then one afternoon, I got a phone call from Amy.

"Just a heads up Rob. Scott will be in town tomorrow for meetings."

After hanging up, I sat there staring out my office window and my thoughts were not nice. Before leaving work, I told my secretary that I had to take the next day off to take care of some personal business. That evening over dinner, Nancy told me that she might have to work late the next day and I made no comment. The next morning, I called Amy at work and asked what Nancy's schedule would normally be.

"Normal day would be a one hour lunch break at noon and then off at five."

"No chance of her working late?"

"We never work late around here Rob."

"Don't tell her I called, okay?"

"Sure enough Rob and good luck."

As I disconnected, I wondered how I should take that "good luck."

At eleven forty-five, I was parked where I could watch the front door of the office building where Nancy worked. At one minute after twelve, Nancy came out the front door on the arm of a man. I was a little surprised to see that he was a good bit older than Nancy's twenty-six. If I had to guess I would put him in his late forties or early fifties.

They walked over to Nancy's car, got in and pulled out of the lot. I started following them and quickly found out that 'tailing' someone isn't as easy as cop shows make it look. Heavy traffic, stupid drivers and lights that were programmed just to fuck you up allowed them to get away from me. I drove back and parked where I could watch Nancy's office again. Amy had told me that lunch was from noon until one, but it was a little after two-thirty when Nancy and the man returned. I left to get a bite to eat, but was back at twenty to five. At five on the dot, Nancy and the man came out, got in her car and drove off. I was right behind them, but I had no better luck than I'd had at lunch time. I lost them before we had gone a mile. I was thinking that I would have been better off in a taxi telling the driver to "Follow that car."

I was sitting on the couch when Nancy got there at nine.

"How was work?"

"A bitch. I hate it when you get last minute projects that have unreasonable deadlines."

I stared at her for several seconds and then asked, "Are you sure that you want to go through with this marriage that's coming up?"

"Of course. Why are you asking me that?"

"I've never talked much about Grace other than to tell you that I caught cheating on me with her boss. But the way I caught her I've never mentioned. What happened was that I caught her in a couple of small lies and that made me suspicious. Then she started working late after a couple of years of never working past five o'clock. Then one day I was in town and near her office and it was close to lunch time, so I thought I'd stop in and take her to lunch. I got there just in time to see her leave her office arm in arm with her boss. That night I asked her what she did for lunch that day and she told me that she was so snowed under with work that she'd had a sandwich at her desk. A flat out lie.

The next day I was outside her building when she left for lunch and I watched her and her boss walk across the street to the Marriot, but they didn't go into the restaurant. They got on the elevator and took it to the sixth floor. I knew the Marriott and I knew that there were no restaurants or coffee shops on the sixth floor – just rooms. I hired a private detective and the rest as they say is history."

"What has that got to do with me being sure that I want to marry you?"

"Apparently you made some enemies when you worked in Atlanta. One of them must be keeping pretty close tabs on you because I got a phone call yesterday telling me that if I wanted to know what a cheating slut you were, I should check out the way you behaved when your old boyfriend was around. I was told that the boyfriend, Scott something or other, would be in town today and it might be to my benefit to check out what you and this Scott guy were up to.

"At first I thought it was bullshit. Just someone you pissed off trying to get back at you. But then you told me that you would be working late tonight. I can count on the thumbs of one foot the number of times you worked late since I have known you. I remembered how it was with Grace so I convinced myself I'd better check things out. I was outside your office when you went to lunch with a guy. Your lunch period is from noon till one, but you didn't come back to work until two-thirty. I was there when you got off work at five and I saw you leave with the same guy you went to lunch with. I'm assuming that it was this Scott character. The bottom line is that you didn't work late and you just lied to me about it. I have no idea where you were from five until you walked in the door a few minutes ago, but I do know that it wasn't at work."

Nancy was silent for a moment and then she said, "I'm sorry."

"Sorry for what?"

"For lying to you. I suppose I should have just told you what I was doing, but I didn't think that you would understand."

"Understand what? That you were going to spend an evening with an old lover? You are right. I wouldn't – don't – understand."

"I didn't spend the evening with an old lover. I spent it with a dear friend who used to be a lover."

And then she told me about going to work in the Atlanta office, being assigned to work with Scott. She said she was young and probably naïve, but she fell in love with Scott. Scott told her that he loved her too and they fell into an affair. After several months, she asked him when he was going to divorce his wife and marry her and he admitted that it would never happen. He loved her more than he loved his wife, but he still loved his wife and children and he wasn't going to give them up.

"I ended my affair with him, but we still had to work together so we stayed friends. He was my mentor and he helped me a lot as far as the job was concerned, but our romance had upset some of the people at the office and I was asked to transfer to some other office.

"I still keep in touch with Scott and when he comes to town, I have lunch with him and sometimes dinner and we talk. That's all we do Rob, talk. He is behind me. All he is to me is a good friend. I guess I should have told you, but again, I just thought that you wouldn't understand.

"So to answer your question Rob, yes I am sure that I want our marriage to happen. I'm sorry for lying to you and I promise that it will never happen again."

To shorten the tale, I believed her and the wedding went off as scheduled.

*****

The next three years were good ones. Nancy still met with Scott for lunch or an occasional dinner when he came to town, and she always told me ahead of time when he was going to be there.

I don't want to give the impression that I sat around fat, dumb, and happy because that wasn't the case. I'd already been burned by an unfaithful wife and as innocent as Nancy made her meetings with Scott seem, there was always a small spot in the back of my mind where suspicion resided. I checked and double checked things when Scott came to town. I checked her clothes in the dirty clothes hamper. I looked through her car and I checked out her purse, but I never found anything even remotely out of line. Not very trusting of me, but I had been burned once and it was something that you never forget.

One night over dinner, Nancy told me that Scott would be in town in two days. "I'd like to bring him home for dinner. I think you two should meet. Would it be alright with you?"

"I don't see why not" I said, but not really meaning it. However it would give me a chance to see how they acted with each other.

Actually the evening went surprisingly well. Scott was a likeable guy and just watching him and Nancy together you would never suspect that once they had been a whole lot more than just friends. But I still couldn't help but wonder. Having been burnt once will do that to you. I excused myself to use the bathroom and as soon as I was in and had the door locked behind me, I went out the window and around the house to where I could look in the dining room window. My thinking was that with me out of the room if there was anything going on between them, Scott wouldn't pass up the opportunity to at least grab a quick feel or a kiss for the thrill of doing it while in my home and with me being close by. But nothing was going on. Nancy and Scott just sat there and talked.

Another two years went by, Scott came to town three or four times a year and most of the time Nancy had him over for dinner. I never saw anything that made me even slightly suspicious, but I still had that teeny-tiny bit of unease in the back of my mind. To me, it just wasn't natural for Nancy and Scott to have the relationship they had after having the torrid sexual affair that Amy had told me about. I had my doubts and yes, even a tad of suspicion, but life with Nancy was good. Actually, it was great so I decided that even if there was something going on what I didn't know wouldn't hurt me.

*****

But then fate or the gods decided that things were going too good to be left alone, so they threw some shit into the game. The owner of the company I work for brought his daughter into the company. Althea was 22 and a recent graduate from the University of Michigan. She was also the spitting image of porn star Austin Kincaid. She was hot! When she walked into a room where I happened to be, everything I had got hard. My tongue got stiff, my cock turned to stone, and even the hairs on my arm got erect and for some strange reason, I was never able to understand Althea set her sights on me. I mean I'm no great shakes. I was your basic, average 36 year old with nothing special going for me and yet a girl 14 years younger decided she wanted me.

Did I want her? Does a ducks ass get wet when it's in the water? Of course I wanted her, but I was a happily married man and I had never fooled around on my wives – either of them – and I wasn't the kind of guy who could. But how do you ignore a walking wet dream who seems determined to get what she wants when what she wants is you?

It started out simple enough. Althea had been there just a little over two months, when one day she sat down at the table where I was taking my morning coffee break.

"How come you don't like me?"

"Who says I don't like you?"

"Well, you are the only man here who hasn't asked me to have lunch with, or stop after work to have a drink with me."

"That doesn't mean that I don't like you. All that means is that I don't want to look foolish."

"How would having lunch with me make you look foolish?"

"Everyone here would be laughing and saying "Look at that old fool trying to hook up with a girl almost young enough to be his daughter.""

"So what? I just happen to prefer older men."

"There is also the little matter that I have a wife."

"It's only lunch or a drink after work. It's not like I'm going to drag you off to my bed. Although the idea does have a certain appeal for me."

"Maybe lunch, but no drink after work. If I were to get a few in me, I might forget you are just a young kid and do something stupid."

"In that case, I'm going to make it my goal to get a half a dozen drinks into you."

"Why?"

"Because you are cute."

That started it. I had lunch with her a couple of times and each time, the talk got more suggestive until one day she flat out asked:

"When are you going to make a serious pass at me?"

"I won't. I am happily married and I won't cheat on my wife."

"Bullhocky! If I stripped right in front of you here and now, you would be on me like a duck on a june bug."

"No I wouldn't" I said even as I knew it was a lie.

"Oh yeah? Well let's just see" she said as she started to unbutton her blouse. I have no idea if she would have taken her blouse off or not, but suddenly our waitress appeared, took one look at what Althea was doing and said:

"Not in here honey. You two need to get a room if you are going to do that sort of thing."

"Saved by the bell" I thought, but I was wrong. Two hours later I was in my office on the phone, when Althea came in. She closed the door behind her and I told her I would be with her in a minute. I went back to my phone conversation and was writing some notes and then I looked up to see that Althea had already taken off her blouse and was in the process of unhooking it. I did the only thing I could think of. I told Mark that something had come up and I'd have to call him back and then I got up and left my office.

Ten minutes later, Althea tracked me down to the break room. "You are no fun" she said.

"I'm a lot of fun in the right place and with the right person. I like my job and I like working here and I would be out of here on my ass, if your father were to ever find out that you were in my office and undressed."

"Who would tell him? I sure wouldn't."

"Why are you doing this Althea?"

"Doing what?"

"Throwing yourself at me. Lord knows that there are plenty of single guys working here tripping over their tongues trying to get to you. Why me?"

"Maybe I like the challenge."

"The challenge?"

"Every guy who works here – a lot of them married – has come sniffing around. Every guy but you."

"I'm spoken for Althea. I'm happily married and that's enough for me."

"Maybe so, but I still like a challenge."

After that, Althea put on her version of a full court press. She looked for opportunities to get me alone and when she did, her behavior was outrageous. In an elevator, she pressed herself into me and rubbed my cock through my pants. In the break room, she lifted her skirt and showed me that no panties covered her clean shaven beaver. She came into my office one rainy day and opened her raincoat to show me that she was naked from the waist up. On my birthday, she gave me a card and when I opened it, I found a picture of her lying naked on a couch. Her legs were spread wide, her hands cupped her tits and the enclosed note said:

"This could be your birthday present."

I'm only human and the constant attentions of a sexy young thing were wearing me down and a couple of times, I almost gave in.

*****

We had a barbecue one Saturday and Glen and Amy were there. I was doing the grill work and making general conversation with Amy, when she asked:

"Everything cool with you and Nancy?"

"Couldn't be better. Why do you ask?"

"Doesn't it bother you, all the time she spends with Scott when he is here?"

"Nah! They are just good friends."

She didn't say any more, but the look she gave me fairly screamed, "Are you brain dead?"

That conversation stayed with me and the next time Scott came to town, I decided to run a little test and hopefully put everything to rest at least as far as that teeny-tiny voice in the back of my head was concerned. As it had become a habit, Nancy invited Scott to dinner. I occasionally got called into to work in the evenings. It didn't happen often, but it did happen enough that my leaving the house after dinner wouldn't seem unusual to Nancy. I set it up with Glen to give me a call around six-thirty. When the call came, I took it and said I'd be right in, kissed Nancy goodbye and left. I drove to work and then called home so Nancy could see from caller ID that I was at work. I told her I would be at least three hours and that she shouldn't bother waiting up for me. Then I settled back in my chair and read the book I had brought with me. At eleven, I went home and found that Nancy was waiting up for me.

"I'm horny lover. No way was I going to be able to sleep until you scratched my itch."

The next day, I took the afternoon off and headed home. I collected the voice activated tape recorders that I had placed around the house and then settled down at the kitchen table with a beer to listen to them. There was nothing on the tapes from the three bedrooms or the kitchen. The dining room tape had our dinner conversation up to my leaving and then general chit-chat until Nancy took my phone call. When she hung up she said:

"Rob won't be home until late, so go have a seat in the living room while I clear the table and put the dishes in the dishwasher."

"Let me help you."

"No. You don't know where anything goes. You would only be in the way and slow me down."

The next tape was from the living room and started when Nancy came in from the kitchen.

"Okay, that's done."

"You said he is going to be late. How late is late?"

"I'm guessing that it will be ten-thirty or eleven."

"That gives us a couple of hours. How about it?"

"You know better than that."

"Why not? We have plenty of time."

"Not on my husband's bed or in his home."

"Oh come on love. We have plenty of time and it is a golden opportunity for us."

"No Scott. Be glad you get the long lunches at the motel. That is all you are going to get so be happy with it or we can just call it quits."

"I don't understand you. You like making love with me and here is a great chance to have a couple of hours."

"I don't make love with you Scott, I fuck you. There is no love involved. I admit that I did think I loved you once, but it turns out it was just youthful infatuation. I didn't find out what love really was until I met Rob."

"If you love him so much why are you still going to bed with me whenever I'm in town?"

"It is my silly way of getting back at your wife."

"My wife? What has my wife got to do with it?"

"You don't know?"

"Obviously not."

"She was the one who got me kicked out of Atlanta."

"How did she do that?"

"She went to John Markham and told him that I was breaking up her marriage, that I was an unhealthy influence on you and that I was turning your head and causing you to do things you would otherwise never do. Then she told him that if he didn't get rid of me, she would sue the company for not enforcing its non-fraternization policy. After I transferred here, she called and bitched because he let me transfer instead of firing me. The only way he was able to get her to back off was to remind her that if he fired me, he would have to fire you also."

"I never knew any of that."

"Well you do now. So you have your wife to thank every time you come to town and get lucky. If it wasn't for her, you wouldn't even get a sniff."

"If that is the way you feel, why don't you want to take advantage of tonight to take another shot at getting back at her?"

"I told you. I love my husband and I will not disrespect him by doing it in his house."

"But…"

"No buts Scott. Accept what you get and be happy with it or we can end it."

There was more, but I'd heard all I needed to hear. I was surprised to find that I wasn't angry or upset. I think it was because deep down inside myself, I'd known all along that the two of them were doing what they had been doing. I'd known and I hadn't done anything to find out for sure one way or the other. I was in love with Nancy. I was happy with Nancy and I was happy with our life together. From what I gathered from the tape, it seemed like Nancy loved me and all Scott was to her was recreational sex with getting some revenge on Scott's wife on the side and he was no threat to me. Nancy spoiled me rotten and our love life was great. So she was taking revenge on Scott's wife. So what? Having one long lunch with Scott three or four times a year. The bottom line was that she always came home to me and she never gave me anything but her best. But – and it was a very big BUT – it was still cheating on me. And the thought made me smile.

*****

It was two days before Althea gave me the opening I was looking for. She came into my office and closed the door behind her.

"I need your opinion on something Rob."

I knew she was going to do something outrageous and I was ready for it. She turned her back to me and said:

"I bought some seamed nylons, but I can't tell if the seams are straight or not." She lifted her skirt and showed me her nyloned legs, garter belt, thong panty, and asked, "Are they straight?"

As soon as she turned her back on me, I was out of my chair and before the word "straight" faded, I had reached past her and locked the door with my right hand while my left pulled my zipper down. I spun her around and bent her over my desk as I said:

"I don't know about your seams sweetie, but something else is straight."

I pushed her thong out of the way, used my knees to spread her legs and poked my cock at her pussy. It took a couple of tries before I found her slit and as I pushed, Althea cried:

"Go easy damn it, I'm not wet down there."

"Tough shit sweetie. You've been coming in here and asking for this for months now. You should have made sure that you were ready for it."

I did go slow as I worked myself into her. "Is this what you wanted sweetie, or have you just been teasing me all these months?"

"I…want…it" she grunted as I pushed my last two inches into her.

"Are you a quiet fuck or a noisy fuck?"

"I…am…a…noisy…slut" she groaned out. "Oh shit Robbie, fuck meeeee."

I pulled my tie off and wadded it up and dropped it on the desk in front of her. "Put that in your mouth and bite down on it. We don't want anyone hearing what's going on in here and running to your daddy."

"Fuck daddy!"

"Oh no my sexy young slut, I'm fucking you."

When we finished and I'd cum, I spun her around and pushed her down on her knees in front of me. She knew what I wanted, and she took me in her mouth and sucked me clean. When she had all the juices off me, she tucked my cock back in my pants and then stood up. She took a hankie out of her purse and as she wiped herself she said, "We do get to do this on a bed don't we?"

"You up for a long lunch?"

"You bet."

"We want to be cool about this, so when you leave for lunch drive down to the Wal-Mart parking lot and park at the south end. I'll pick you up there and we will go find a motel."

*****

For the next nine months, Althea and I averaged one 'over the desk' and two 'long lunches' a week. Frankly, it surprised me. I thought for sure that once Althea had gotten what she wanted – met her challenge and won – she would move on to someone younger, but she was pushing for more and more. She even wanted to know when I was going to dump Nancy, so I could spend some more time with her. That was an interesting conversation, that it showed that Althea was no dummy. When she first asked the question, my answer was:

"Why would I want to do that?"

"She's cheating on you so why wouldn't you?"

"Why would you think she is cheating on me?"

"Oh come on Rob. For months it was "No way Althea. I love my wife. I'm happily married and I won't cheat on her" and then 'wam' you've got me bent over your desk. The only way a straight arrow like you would change that quick was if your loving wife was giving some loving to someone else. So when are you going to dump her, so I can move in?"

I had no intention of getting rid of Nancy, but I wanted to hang on to Althea for a little while longer, so I told her it would take a while before I could confront Nancy.

"I have some financial arrangements I need to make and I need to protect some other assets so she doesn't clip me too bad in the divorce. It will be a while. And what's with the "so I can move in" stuff?"

"You do know that I am going to marry you, right?"

"No Althea, I didn't know that."

"Get used to the idea Rob. Now that I've got you, I'm not letting you get away."

That would be a problem down the road, but I would cross that bridge when I came to it. Did I feel guilty over the number of times I'd had sex with Althea? Not really. Granted, I was doing Althea because Nancy was doing Scott, but Nancy only did Scott on one long lunch break three or four times a year while I was nailing Althea three and four times a week. I justified it by saying that I was playing 'catch up' for the years Nancy had been doing Scott. Another reason I didn't feel guilty, was because I planned on confronting Nancy and when I did, I would confess what I'd done with Althea.

Actually, my plan was to let Nancy do the confronting. Why choose a confrontation when I really didn't mind that Nancy saw Scott occasionally? Because I didn't like the sneaking around aspect of it. Also, there was the little matter of "lying." When Nancy and I had our little talk way back when we were still living together and I confronted her over her meeting with Scott, she told me that she would never lie to me again. And while she might have said "yes" if I flat out asked her if she was fucking Scott, she just told me that all they did when he came to town was have lunch, it was a lie and it bothered me. Of course she could try to weasel her way around it because what she had said was that "Scott and I take our lunch hour together." Not "have lunch" but take their lunch hour at the same time and spend it together. Whatever! I wanted it all out in the open. She could have her time with Scott and I'd play with Althea, but there would be no secrets, no sneaking around and no lies.

*****

During the nine months that Althea and I were playing, Scott came to town twice. Both times, thanks to Nancy's "Scott will be in town tomorrow so can I have him over for dinner?" I was able to have a private detective in place to follow them. Both times, they left work at lunch time and drove to the Days Inn on Walnut and Third and stayed there until two-thirty. Nancy made love to me both nights when we went to bed. I often wondered if she showered at the motel or if I was getting sloppy seconds if I was I doubted that she was doing it for a kick, since she made love with me four and five times a week anyway. Although the nights we made love after she'd been with Scott, did seem to be a little more intense and I wondered if that was because she felt guilty and needed to make it up to me.

I finally decided it was time to bring things out into the open and when Nancy told me that Scott would be in town the next day, I was ready. The next day, I told Althea we were going to take a long lunch. At ten after twelve, I called the Days Inn and asked if Nancy Barton or Scott Clardon had checked in yet and I was told that yes, Mr. Clardon had checked in. I told them I wanted to send him flowers and asked for his room number. I was told he was in room 117 and I thanked the desk clerk and hung up.

When Althea and I got to the Days Inn, I saw Nancy's car parked in front of room 117 and luckily there were no cars on either side of her. I pulled in and parked on the driver's side of her Honda Accord and then I went and asked for a room and specifically asked for 115 or 119. I was given room 115 and Althea and I went inside and proceeded to get all sweaty and out of breath. I had to admit I get a kick out, doing Althea while Nancy was right next door. Althea had no idea what I was doing, but there was no doubt in my mind that if she had known, she would have been kicking the wall and screaming out my name loud enough for Nancy to have heard it through the walls.

Althea and I stayed in the room until three. I knew that Nancy left between two-fifteen and two-thirty and I didn't want to run into her coming out of Scott's room. It was enough for Nancy to see my pick-up truck parked next to her. She couldn't miss it. It had a custom paint job with hand applied pin striping and had "Rob" lettered on the driver's door and Nancy lettered on the passenger door. She could not possibly miss it and when she did, she would know that I knew what she was doing. Or then again maybe she wouldn't. Her car was a Honda Accord and it looked like a thousand other Hondas and maybe she would think that I hadn't recognized the car as being hers. The confrontation would play out at home when she brought Scott home for dinner.

Things do not always go as planned.

I arrived home to find Nancy loading suitcases into her car. Scott was nowhere in sight, so I guessed that she had dropped him at his hotel.

"What are you doing?"

"I'm loading my clothes in the car."

"I can see that so the question is why are you doing it?"

"Because I won't live with a cheating asshole."

"You won't live with a cheater? You're kidding, right?"

"No I'm not! I was driving down Walnut and I saw your truck in the Days Inn parking lot so I pulled over and sat there and watched it. I saw you come out of room 115 with that slut, so I'm leaving you."

In that instant, everything changed. She had been cheating on me for over six years and now she was getting on her high horse with me? She was leaving me because I was a cheater? Well fuck her! I turned away from her and headed for the house.

"What? You aren't going to say anything?"

"You want me to say something? Okay. Good riddance."

"What the hell does that mean?"

"Just that. Goodbye and good riddance."

I walked away from her and into the house. Two minutes later, she was in the house and fuming. "You have some nerve talking to me like that just because I caught you cheating on me with some floozy."

"You didn't catch me cheating you stupid cunt! I caught you. You "just happened' to see my truck as you were driving down Walnut? Bullshit! You saw my truck because it was parked right next to your Honda when you came out of room 117 where you had been with Scott since twelve-ten."

Her face lost all of its color when I said that.

"My truck was parked next to you so you would know you were busted. The woman you saw me coming out of the room with was the woman from the detective agency who was operating the recording equipment that taped you and "your good friend" Scott hanging horns on me. And you can tell that asshole that I will make damned sure that his wife gets a copy of everything I have. I'll also send a copy to John Markham and maybe this time he will enforce the no fraternization rule and if not, maybe this time Scott's wife will follow through on her threat to sue. Your bags are packed and loaded so get your sorry ass out of my sight."

She started to leave and then she turned and said, "What are you going to do?"

"Stupid question Nancy. I'm going to divorce you and my grounds will be infidelity. Now please get the fuck out of here."

Nancy called me three days later. "I'm sorry for the way I acted Rob. I don't know what came over me. I love you Rob. Is there some way we can get by this?"

"Not a prayer Nancy. When I came home that day, I was going to sit down and talk with you and try to work something out. I loved you enough to want to get by it, but when you hit me with that shit about not living with a cheating asshole after you had been cheating on me for over six years, you ended it. Please don't call me again."

She did call two days after she was served. "I won't contest the divorce if you promise not to tell Scott's wife or John Markham."

"You have no leverage Nancy. You can contest it all you want, but it will still eventually happen."

"Yes, but if I fight it, it will drag out and cost you more."

"You have no grounds to contest it with Nancy."

"The lawyer I talked to says I do."

"And they would be what?"

"I remember the conversation I had with Scott about his wife, John Markham and the no fraternization clause. It happened years ago. According to my lawyer since you kept exercising your conjugal rights after finding out about me and Scott, you in effect forgave me."

"Where did you find this lawyer; riding on the back bumper of an ambulance? It is a case of "he said/she said" Nancy. I confronted you and you promised that it would never happen again. I forgave you, but then you went out and cheated again and this time, I'm not forgiving you. That's going to be my story and you can say it is false all you want, but I'm the one with the private detective's reports and recordings, so who are they going to believe?

"As far as letting the asshole off the hook, it is never going to happen. He has been fucking you behind my back for over six years. I owe that cocksucker. I won't send anything to John Markham because you will need a job to support yourself, but it is going to be up to your asshole lover to keep his wife from going to see Markham."

It was a bluff and fortunately Nancy bought it. She didn't contest the divorce and I didn't have to produce the non-existing recording of what went on in room 117 that day and Nancy never challenged me on my statement that Althea was there as an employee of the detective agency.

I don't know what went on between Scott and his wife, but I did send her copies of everything that I had. All I know is that Nancy still has her job although Amy tells me that she doesn't talk to Scott on the phone anymore and Scott never comes to town anymore either.

*****

Althea got her wish. She did marry me and I do have to say that marrying the boss's daughter is a great career move. I've had two promotions in the year we have been married. To add to that, I got to go home and spend my nights with a woman who looks like a porn star and who seems to want to fuck me to death.

Althea made it clear to me that she will cut my dick off, if I even think of trying on another woman and I made sure that she knew I would kick her to the curb in a heartbeat if she ever cheats on me.

Do I regret the way things turned out? Yes I do. I was in love with Nancy and I was happy with Nancy. Happy enough that I was even willing to let her have her part-time lover, as long as everything was out in the open, but she came home to me and kept on spoiling me rotten.

Althea would not have lasted too much longer, not because I didn't care for her because I did. It was just that I cared for Nancy more, and there isn't any way that I could have kept on taking care of the both of them. Nancy killed things when she decided that her cheating was okay, but if I cheated it wasn't okay.

In retrospect, we would probably still be together if I hadn't gotten "cute" and taken Althea to the motel that day. If I would have just confronted her at dinner that night, we probably would have worked things out. Oh well, what is that they say? That hindsight is always twenty-twenty?

~~The End~~

Also by this Author:

Erotica Short Stories, Vol. 8 –

(Wild Urges)

A Weird One

From the Author

If you enjoyed any of my books then please share the love and promote my books in Amazon.

If you write me a review and send me an email I will send you a free book, or many.
(Just know that these emails are filtered by my publisher.)

Good news is always welcome.

One Last Thing, For Kindle Readers...

When you turn the page, Kindle will give you the opportunity to rate this book and share your thoughts on Facebook and Twitter. If you enjoyed my writings, would you please take a few seconds to let your friends know about it? Because... when they enjoy they will be grateful to you and so will I.

Thank You!

An Open Letter from Just Plain Bob

A message for those who like my stories, those who hate my stories, those who are indifferent and those who have yet to make up their minds.

I have often stated that I really don't care what others think about my stories, that I write for my own enjoyment and then I offer to share. If you like my stories fine and if you don't, also fine since I have already satisfied my target audience - me!

It is human nature to strive to get better. If you take up bowling your first games are going low scoring, but you will work and practice to get better and as your average climbs you may forget the game where you had three gutter balls and shot an eighty-six, but that game is still there in your past.

Your first time on the golf course you shot an eighty on the front nine, but did you settle for that being your game or did you work to improve? You may eventually get a three handicap, but that nine hole eighty is still there as part of your past.

When you hired in at your job did you say, "Cool, I got it made" and do nothing more than what you barely had to do or did you go to work thinking that, "Someday I'm going to be running this place." You might never climb that high, but human nature says that you are going to at least try.

It is the same with authors who write stories and post them on sites like Literotica. Their first stories might not be all that good, but comments and feedback along with a desire to get better drive them toward putting out a better product or to at least try.

I'm no different. My first stories might not have been all that great, but they are still there on the hard drive. I like cheating wife stories and five years ago I found my first adult site that catered to cheating wife stories. It was a pay site, but it had a policy of giving a free lifetime membership to anyone who submitted five stories to the site. How hard can that be I said to myself as I sat down and fired up the word processor and went to work.

I sent my five stories in and sat back to enjoy my free membership and a funny thing happened. I started getting feedback, most of it positive, and I became hooked. I started cranking out more stories. The site I was sending my stories to had seven categories:

Bisexual
Cream Pie

Groups
I Watch
Gang Bang
Racial
SM/BD

I know nothing about bisexual or SM/BD and I had no interest in Groups so all the stories I wrote I tailored for the four remaining categories:

Cream Pie
I Watch
Gang Bang
Racial.

I turned out eight stories a month, two for each category, which means that after five years I have over 120 stories in each of those categories and they are all still on the hard drive.

A year ago I received an email asking me why I never posted stories on Literotica. The answer? I didn't know about Lit. I pulled it up, liked what I saw, and started sending in stories to it. All new stories? No, not hardly, not with over 400 stories sitting on the hard drive. Maybe one new story for each fifteen or so old ones. The newer ones are better, at least I think they are and I have received some feedback that leads me to believe that others think so too, and I will continue to write new ones.

But I am still going to recycle what is on the hard drive, stories that were written specifically to fit the four categories. That means that those of you who hate cream pie stories still have eighty or so to look forward to. Ditto for those who call me a racist; you will get another seventy or so interracial stories.

Those who hate wimps will only see about fifty more of those because the stories I sent to the I Watch category were split 50/50 between what some call wimps and some call "real men." Why the 50/50 split? It came from listening to the readers. I would get feedback asking me why all the men in my stories were hard asses. "In real life men are more forgiving, especially if it is the first indiscretion." So I would write stories with forgiving husbands and boyfriends and then the next batch of feedback would say, "Why are all your husbands spineless wimps" and I'd write stories that went back the other way.

Eventually I came to realize that I was wasting my time - there was no way I could write a story that would satisfy everybody and that is when I adopted my philosophy of writing for my own enjoyment and then offering to share.

As far as the gangbang stories? Well, what can I say? Gangbangs are gangbangs and there are still eighty or so of them to go.

The bottom line is that Literotica readers are going to see more of my old stories than my new ones. If I'm still around three or four years from now it will probably go the other way, more new than old.

I feel the need to respond to some of the comments and emails I have received. By far the largest percentage comes from people who say, "You are an asshole because all women are not whores and sluts and that's all you make them out to be."

Next most common is, "You must really hate women you sick fuck."

"You must be a wimp because all the men in your stories are wimps" is up there in the top ten along with, "Why don't you give it a rest and go crawl off in a hole somewhere."

There is a lot more, but I'm only going to address those four and in reverse order.

I won't stop and go crawl in a hole because I am enjoying the hell out of what I am doing and remember what I said, I am doing this for MY OWN ENJOYMENT and then I offer to share. Some obviously like my sharing with them and so I will continue to do so. No one is holding a gun to a reader's head and telling them they must click on a Just Plain Bob story or die. It is a conscious choice on the reader's part to move that mouse and click on that story.

When a man finds out he has a cheating wife or girlfriend there are only a limited number of ways he can handle it. If he loves her he can forgive, try to forget and try to hold on and somehow make things work. He can turn his back on her, walk away and get on with his life. The third option is to take revenge.

According to a good portion of those who send me feedback the first and second options are proof that the men are wimps. If the man takes the third option he is still considered a wimp if he doesn't do some sort of physical damage to the woman and her lover. These readers believe that the only way not to be a wimp is to kill, maim and destroy everything in sight. Doing that however, will invariably get the man throw in jail and that is why it so rarely happens in real life.

In real life most revenge takes place in the man's head when he says to himself, "I should have _____ (fill in the blank) the fucking cunt!" I know this because I have been there and done that (see The Dark Trilogy). In my stories I try to mirror real life so kill, maim and destroy are going to be for the most part absent. Outside of some fisticuffs there will be very little physical violence in my stories. Most of my husbands are going to do what I did, what several of my friends and others that I know have done, forgive, or walk away. If this makes them wimps and me a wimp for writing the story that way, so be it.

Next is the "I must hate all women." Nothing could be farther from the truth. I love women. I lust after women. I even like whores and sluts. I have been married four times, engaged two other times (that did not end in marriage) and I have always had girlfriends between marriages. My philosophy is that women were put on this earth for me to enjoy and I'm not talking just sexually. I could sit at the mall (and have) for hours and just girl watch.

The engagements, girlfriends and three of the four marriages bring me to the #1 anti JPB comment on the list.

"You are an asshole because all women aren't whores and sluts."

Well dear reader, you can not prove that by me! I will say up front that I KNOW all women aren't whores and sluts, BUT the majority of the women in my life were. My mother ran around on my father for years while he was driving a truck for a living. My Aunt Margaret cheated regularly on my Uncle Bill, as did my Aunt Mildred on my Uncle Paul. My Aunt Betty fucked around on my Uncle Bob for years and finally left him for his brother, my Uncle Wendell. Uncle Wendell in turn caught her on her knees at his company Christmas party giving Season's Greetings to his boss.

My sister is three times divorced and each divorce came about when the then current husband caught her out spreading pollen. Both of the engagements I mentioned ended when I found out that I was not the one and only and a lot of the girls I dated between marriages never made it to engagement status for the same reason.

And that brings me to my three ex-wives. The first one, Helen (I believe I commented on her in the intro to The Dark Trilogy) had seven different lovers before I found out what was going on. I was living proof that love is blind. Ditto with my second wife. She had a secret life that she hid from me and when I found out about her brother, his friends and the gangbangs she was history.

My third marriage ended in divorce because of a different kind of cheating (and I can just imagine the outrage I am going to get over this) - she cheated on me with an idea. I was away from home on business, she was lonely, a couple of Jehovah's Witnesses knocked on the door and my wife, with nothing better to do invited them in. When I came home from my trip I found out that she had found God. On a scale that runs from TRUE BELIEVER on one end to ATHEIST on the other you will find me just to the right of AGNOSTIC and since I would not allow myself to be SAVED the marriage eventually died.

So yes, I write about sluts and whores because as everyone knows, you tend to write about the things you know. And I do like sluts and whores, just not the ones that lie to me and cheat on me.

So be forewarned - if you click on a Just Plain Bob story you will be getting sluts, whores and husbands who do not kill, maim and destroy. There are other things you will rarely find in a Just Plain Bob story. Even though I try to mirror real life my stories all take place in StoryLand. In StoryLand STDs and un-wanted pregnancies do not exist unless the author feels like they may add something to the story. Bad things do not happen in StoryLand unless the author so wills it and no amount of "You should have…" in comments and feedback will change a story already posted.

Lastly, I will touch on a truth. None of what I have written here means shit because the same readers will still read the same stories that they profess to hate and make the same comments they have always made. Knowing this, I will deliberately post stories that will have them frothing at the mouth.

It is the least I can do for an adoring public.

Thank you!

Just Plain Bob
justplainbob@awesomeauthors.org